Edward Conway Jones

'76 Lyrics of the Revolution

Edward Conway Jones

'76 Lyrics of the Revolution

ISBN/EAN: 9783744784313

Printed in Europe, USA, Canada, Australia, Japan

Cover: Foto ©Andreas Hilbeck / pixelio.de

More available books at **www.hansebooks.com**

'76

Lyrics of the Revolution

By

Rev. Edward C. Jones, A.M.

Philadelphia

Mdcccxcix

IN MEMORY

OF

MY BELOVED FATHER

" My country, 'tis of thee,
  Sweet land of liberty,"
    Of thee I sing."

PREFACE

THIS volume is intended for the patriotic people of America, who hold in grateful remembrance the memory of those who fought the battles, framed the Constitution, and administered the government in the early days of our country.

Time should not lessen this feeling of interest and pride in our forefathers, but it should be kept alive ; and it is the hope of the publisher that this little book may assist in keeping bright the spark that influenced the Revolutionary patriots.

That the Revolutionary period is still regarded with pride is shown by the recent interest in the hereditary patriotic societies of the land, having for their foundation the love for and history of the heroic age of our republic.

The poems presented were written almost half

a century ago, and have been selected as the most interesting of a large collection.

May they awaken in the reader the patriotic fervor of the author.

CONTENTS

Contents

'76

Lyrics of the Revolution

★ ★ ★

GENERAL JOSEPH WARREN.*

THE Old South Church, where Freedom swung
   Her censer full and free,
And Warren's bold, untrammelled tongue
On despots' ears its changes rung,
   Our bosom warms to thee.

Along the aisle the scarlet coats,
   Ranged in a phalanx deep,
But fearless rolled the master notes,
And in the tide an atom floats,
   The blades which dare not leap.

---

* General Joseph Warren delivered an oration in the Old South Church, of Boston, when the British bayonets guarded the very pulpit. He fell afterwards at Bunker Hill.

From that old guarded pulpit height,
  Where glows the bristling steel,
Beams forth a never-fading light,
The ray of truth and conscious right,
  And millions toward it kneel.

What is the bayonet to him,
  Who, girt with justice stern,
Peals to the heaven his freedom hymn,
And rallies hearts, and eyes now dim
  Bids with emotion burn?

What is to him the banded force,
  With glitter all bedight?
If checked the lightning in its course,
If lulled by threat the billow hoarse,
  Then arms his soul may fright.

But while a man he stands unawed,
  Save by his Maker's frown,
As mounts the lark from dewy sod,
His spirit soars to truth and God,
  Nor minions cast it down.

On Bunker's battled height there stood,
  He who that pulpit graced ;
The beautiful, the true, the good,
Sealed what he uttered with his blood,
  Nor run that blood to waste.

For millions caught the patriot glow,
From mountain-top to dale,
And dealt a more than iron blow,
And hailed a despot's overthrow,
While we rehearse the tale.

PATRICK HENRY.

"Our chains are forged ; their clanking may be heard
on the plains of Boston ; the next gale may bring to our
ears the clash of resounding arms."

VIEW that eagle eye,—that brow,
Seeming God illumined now ;
Watch that sinewy arm, whose sweep
Is the gauge of feeling deep ;
Hear those words of forceful aim,
Every syllable a flame :

"They have forged our massy chains,
Clank they now on Boston's plains,
And the gale may shortly bring
News of Freedom's suffering ;
Freighted now that gale may be
With deep tones of misery.
Iron heel is on our shore,
Myrmidons come thronging o'er,

Quartered on us as of old,
Wolf has ever watched the fold.
See them march with pompous tread !
Rush-like, shall we bow the head ?
Yield our heaven-born rights because
'Tis a crown that issues laws !
Higher than the Crown arise
Human hopes and liberties ;
All its jewels in a blaze,
Cast no shade on Freedom's rays.
Streaming from yon upper dome,
Come, supernal radiance, come !
Light us onward, beacon-fire !
And, as on a funeral pyre,
Wrong, yes, chartered wrong, shall be
Nought but ashes to the free.
Brothers, talk not now of peace ;
Let such fond delusion cease.
When ye heard that booming gun,
Far away in Lexington,
When arose the sulphur wreath,
Telling heroes fought beneath,
Concord took another name,
And baptized afresh became.
They are fiery pillars now ;
By them guided, seal your vow,
Look to Concord, Lexington !
See the foe retreating then,
And if ye no throbbing feel,

If your arm no strength reveal,
If your proud, dilating soul,
Spurneth not all base control,
Manhood from the brow erase,
And in dust conceal your face !
God of Hosts ! appeal to Thee
Those who pant for liberty !
Here, among our breezy hills,
Here, beside our dancing rills,
Here, where broad savannas sweep,
Swords, like flames, shall fiercely leap,
Hills, and streams, and plains shall be
Only ours—and we be free !"

GAGE AND WASHINGTON.

Twenty years had elapsed since General Washington
and General Gage had fought side by side on the bloody
battle-field of the Monongahela. The one was now
obeying the commands of his sovereign, the other up-
holding the cause of an oppressed people.—JARED
SPARKS.

'TWAS summer morn ! A gallant band,
  With arms of burnished steel,
Marched by the river's side, inspired
  By war's awakening peal,
While on the left the forest deep
Was startled from its ancient sleep.

13

'Twas summer eve ! That gallant band,
  With half its number slain,
A panic-stricken remnant, fled,
  And crossed the stream again ;
For Braddock's sun was darkened now,
And death-dew on his writhing brow.

Conversing low, two youthful forms
  Upon that eve were seen,
When French and Indian poured the fire
  From deep and dark ravine ;
When battle-cloud had rolled away,
Among the living still were they.

Beneath the one two noble steeds
  Had fallen in the fray ;
The other, leading on the van,
  Stood hero-like that day ;
Knit in the bonds of friendship there,
When shall they meet again, and *where ?*

Pass twenty years ; on Bunker Hill
  The contest rages now,
And men aggrieved with wrong are there
  To ratify their vow ;
But sternly as they kept their trust,
Freedom's dear ensign trailed in dust.

Hope on, hope ever, one there comes
  To head his country's force ;
Trust him to breast the tide that sweeps
  Its desolating course.
At Braddock's side he played the man ;
Still is he first in glory's van.

On Boston's heights a freeman's camp
  Held that majestic form ;
He grasps his pen, and, as he writes,
  His pensive features warm ;
He thinks of one who near him stood
Where rolled Monongahela's flood.

To him he wrote, the leader here
  Of yonder British band,
Now pouring death on humble hearts
  At sovereignty's command, —
Here, when the first great strife was o'er,
Met Gage and Washington once more !

SERGEANT JASPER.

"On the 28th of June, 1776, the British fleet advanced against the fort on Sullivan's Island (Fort Moultrie). The engagement began about eleven o'clock in the fore-noon, and lasted till seven in the evening. In this obsti-nate engagement the flagstaff of the fort was shot away; but Sergeant Jasper leaped down upon the beach, snatched the flag, fastened it to a sponge-staff, and, while the ships were directing their broadsides upon the fort, mounting the merlon, replaced the flag."

SHINING through the battle-wreath
　　Like a meteor gay,
Catching glances, firing hearts,
　　Waved the flag that day;
Swifter than the meteor shoots
　　From its airy dome,
Rapid as descending bird
　　To its nest would come,
To the beach the staff now went,
Toppling from the battlement.

How the galling cannonade
　　Heaved the water's breast!
But a granite giant stood
　　In its tranquil rest;
And the good old fort returned
　　All its deadlier hail,
Till amid the lurid glare
　　Parker's cheek was pale,

For 'tis rebels who compete
With Britannia's noble fleet.

But the flag ! it must not lie
   In dishonored state ;
Made to wave against the sky,
   Like a soul elate,
Catching purer breath from heaven,
   As from dust it soars,
Is there one who to its height
   That dear flag restores ?
Heroes ! wash its dust away !
Was it made to kiss the clay ?

"Symbol of my country's hope,"—
   Thus one patriot cried,—
"Formed beneath yon azure cope,
   Yet to wave our pride,
Here, within the bomb-shell's range,
   Leap I to the beach ;
Guardian angel of the fort,
   Still within my reach,
Ne'er did diver in the sea
Plunge for pearl so pure as thee !"

He has gained it, and his brow
   All the soul reveals ;
Up the merlon ! Jasper, now,
   Up, amid the peals

From thy comrades' lips which come,
  And, while there, oh, place
In its stony keep the flag
  Which has spurned disgrace !
See ! it floats again !   Brave heart,
Thou hast played a Roman part !

Deeds there are which to the soul
  Come like bursts of song,
Deeds which from the days of yore
  Sweep like chant along ;
Deeds which stir the blood, though old,
  Light the dullest eye ;
Deeds which bear thy broadest stamp,
  ·Immortality !
One of such deeds, by blest decree,
Was, Jasper, thus reserved for thee.

THE BATTLE OF LONG ISLAND AND THE RETREAT.

  The historical facts embodied in this lyric are from
Frost's " History of the United States," pages 219-221.

A LENGTHENED line of bravest hearts stood on
    that island fair,
'Twas August eve, and sultriness was brooding in
    the air ;

18

He reined his charger, he their chief, who on them
    leaned for aid,
And bared to heaven his brow serene, and paused
    but once, and said :

"Soldiers ! a brilliant host encamps upon this
    fragrant sod,
Clinton and Cornwallis, and Grant, shall give but
    once the nod,
When all the hireling Hessian band, and veterans
    of the Crown,
Shall sweep the keenest scythe of war to mow the
    rebels down.
Say, when their demon shout of joy reverberates
    the hill,
Will ye, with hearts of oak, support and trust your
    leader still?"

A solemn hush, then from the line went up a
    thunder peal,
It rolled across the meadows, pierced Flatbush
    wooded height,
And Percy heard the echo deep that glorious,
    August night :
"Will ye, with hearts of oak, support and trust
    your leader still?"
'Twas Washington who breathed the words,—
    'twas freemen said, "We will !"

*   *   *   *   *   *   *

The din of contest ceased,—the moon was in an
  August sky,—
And Washington beheld with grief his heroes
  round him lie,
Woodhull and Stanley, captives now, and Sullivan
  the strong,
Long Island saw them true to right, will Heaven
  avenge the wrong?
Two thousand wounded, prisoners, slain, their
  words were with him still,
And yet like music to his soul came that stern vow,
  " We will !"

" We must retreat, the panting hare must lead the
  hound astray,
The lion couches in his lair, we cheat him of his prey ;
We must retreat, a lessened band, in silence and
  in tears,
This grassy shore, Sahara-like, to my dim eye ap-
  pears ;
The field-flower blushes with our blood, its native
  modest blue,
Which spoke of peace and safety once, now hides
  itself from view ;
And sleeping by these rifted pines, and through
  those meadows wide,
Are truest, bravest, kindest men, my treasure and
  my pride.
They fell amid a burst of blaze, their faces to the foe,

Compeers of Greeks at Marathon, in ages long
    ago,
And as long as Memory holds her sway, 'till Death
    this heart shall still,
Will come to cheer me, and to bless, their Spartan
    shout,—" We will !"

MARQUIS DE LA FAYETTE.

This young French nobleman presented himself to Dr. Franklin, and afterwards to the other commissioners, and offered his services as a volunteer. " We cannot," said they, " in conscience urge you to proceed. We possess not the means nor the credit for procuring a vessel for your passage." " Then," exclaimed the gallant youth, " I will provide my own."—*Frost's History*, page 230.

THY vineyards, oh ! my sunny land, are beautiful
    to see,
Thy noble Seine rolls on in pride, with waters
    glad and free,
But far across the ocean's breast I hear the notes
    of woe,
And a voice sinks deep within my heart, whose
    burden still is, " Go !"
Beside thee, oh ! my cherished one, at eventide I
    stand,
And kiss thy ruby lips in love, and clasp thy lily
    hand,

But through my veins, like lava-tide, what stronger
　　currents flow,
For e'en affection's plea is dumb before that man-
　　date, "Go!"
Across the waves a blade of steel fair Freedom
　　holds to me,
Its temper'd edge at feast, and court, and hearth-
　　stone bright I see ;
That blade my hand is pledged to wield, that tem-
　　per'd edge to prove,
To Washington and Liberty I consecrate my
　　love.
Here, in the flush of opening life, from rank and
　　ease I haste
The soldier's rugged toil to share,—the soldier's
　　meal to taste.
The camp-fire and the bivouac, the muster and the
　　march ;
The bugle-blast, the battle-shock, beneath heaven's
　　shrouded arch ;
Be these my future scenes, be this the warp and
　　woof of life.
A brother to the poor oppressed, I join them in
　　the strife,
I claim with them alliance, I hail them kith and
　　kin ;
I bind their bleeding hearts to mine, to suffer or to
　　win.

*　　*　　*　　*　　*　　*　　*

A ship is out upon the deep ; beneath its canvas
    fold
There muses one, how young in years, in stern
    resolve how old !
Still to the western shore he turns, oh ! land him
    safely there,
And consummate his fondest wish, fulfil his dear-
    est prayer.
O Ocean, chain thy tempest now, restrain thy
    sterner mood,
And bid thy softest breezes waft the beautiful, the
    good ;
For never to thy charge was given a brighter gem
    than he,
Who rends the strongest ties of love to battle
    with the free.

*   *   *   *   *   *   *

A bright September day beheld a contest long
    and stern,
The youthful nobleman was there, his battle-task
    to learn ;
And 'mid the iron hail he stood and cheered his
    fainting men,
Inspired with hope the faltering ranks and rallied
    them again ;
A wound he bears, but, heedless all, he presses
    onward yet,
And Freedom here accepts thy blood, thou gallant
    Lafayette ;

Around thy brow unfading wreaths America shall
    twine,
And think of thee with throbbing heart, of thee
    and Brandywine.

STARK, OF BENNINGTON.

    The Americans took four brass field-pieces, one thou-
sand muskets, nine hundred swords, and four baggage-
wagons, a very seasonable supply.—*Frost's History.*

PUSH on the column, Colonel Baum, with wary
    step and sure,
Push on the column, Colonel Baum, with Indian
    scouts before,
And show your German blood to-day, and let the
    war-whoop tell
That savage bands with tomahawks can do my
    bidding well ;
The flour and corn of Bennington, so snugly
    packed away,
Shall have Burgoyne for owner before the close of
    day.

With stealthy tread, a hundred strong, the feath-
    ered Indians go,
And Baum, with half a thousand, brings up the
    rear as slow ;

With wain, and black-mouthed cannon, and ensign
    in the breeze,
They come, ye brave Green Mountain boys, your
    garnered hoard to seize.

But Starke had heard about you, Baum, and the
    patriot sternly said,
That rebel corn and flour will make a *stony kind*
    of bread ;
Yes, Starke has got the warning, and if you still
    persist,
An iron mill will do the work, and you shall be the
    grist.
That corn and flour are dear to him as silver from
    the mine,
And, oh ! Burgoyne, keep cool to-day, it never
    shall be thine.

Throw up your breastwork, Colonel Baum, and
    give your cannon play,
For Freedom's rusty firelocks will match you well
    to-day ;
New Hampshire's plain militia and Warner's regi-
    ment,
When fighting for "the children's bread," will
    surely not relent ;
Throw up your breastwork, Colonel Baum, for it
    will be your last,
As came upon Assyrian host that mystic angel-
    blast ;

So on thy forces, and on thee, the whirlwind shall
    descend,
And here upon the rebel soil thy brief career must
    end.

*   *   *   *   *   *   *

They count the spoils of victory with bosoms
    beating strong,
And every brazen field-piece is honored with a
    song ;
Around the swords and muskets, like joyous boys
    they press,
Theirs is an El Dorado mine of hope and happi-
    ness.
And while the captured foe look on, with sad and
    altered mien,
They pipe a gleesome roundelay upon the trodden
    green ;
.Like maiden at the placid brook, which mirrors all
    her charms,
They thrill with exultation at the noble stand of
    arms,
And cheer the gallant chieftain who led their forces
    on,
And canonized the very dust of good old Ben-
    nington,
Who proved to British veterans the rusty firelocks'
    power,
And kept within his lion gripe *his country's corn
    and flour.*

VALLEY FORGE.

Their line of march from White Marsh to Valley Forge might have been traced by the blood from the bare and mangled feet of the soldiers.—*Frost's History.*

OUR path is traced by a crimson stain,
We leave our mark on the snow-clad plain,
As onward to Valley Forge we press,
Where all will be bleak and verdureless.

Our wives are sighing by hearthstones drear,
Our babes are sobbing and we not near,
The tempest raves through the rifted wood,
And Grief keeps time in her wildest mood.

We go with the axe our huts to raise,
And then to creep to the camp-fire's blaze,
And talk, as our heartstrings closer twine,
Of comrades we lost at Brandywine.

We will know what Famine means, and wish
For the nook of home and the smoking dish ;
And our aching limbs, as they shrink with cold,
Will feel how scant is the garment's fold.

Our path is traced by a ruddy dye,
But we turn our thoughts to the distant sky,
And the snow-clad plain seems a vernal sod,
When we feel our cause is the cause of God.

27

The foe will lodge in the city gay,
And Howe and his troops keep cares away,
And the feast and the dance will loudly tell
How St. George's sons hold carnival.

But we in the rude-built huts will wait
For a brighter day and a nobler fate ;
And, as clings to the sire the trusting son,
We will nestle close to our Washington.

Our path is traced by a crimson stain,
Our blood pours out like the April rain,
But a Spartan heart and an iron will
Shall be the portion of freemen still.

Then, brothers, on to the forest wild,
Let the axes ring,—be the timber piled,—
• The cheek of the Briton will burn with shame
When Valley Forge has a deathless name.

WASHINGTON CROSSING THE DELA-WARE.

On the evening of the 25th of December he crossed the Delaware, marched all night, attacked the Hessians, who had not the slightest intelligence of his approach, and routed them with great slaughter. Colonel Rahl could not resist the impetuous attack, directed, as it was, by Washington in person. And while one thousand of their best troops remained prisoners of war, Washington recrossed to his camp, with the loss of but nine of his men.—*Frost's History.*

No sleep to-night, for through the ice
  The boats must push their way,
And, landing on the farther shore,
  Our black-mouthed cannon play.

The snow and sleet, to beating hearts,
  Bring nought of grief or gloom ;
Hope's heaven-born flower, on Christmas-eve,
  Shall burst in vernal bloom.

With forces spread, they sleep secure,
  While we are drifting nigh.
Ah ! how our victor shout will peal
  Beneath the wintry sky !

No sleep to-night ; an icy path
  Conducts us to the foe ;
And Rahl, let once the morning break,
  The rebels' might shall know.

Silent as shadows o'er the lea,
   Stern as an Alpine hill,
Banded as Macedonian force,
   Calm as the noiseless rill ;

Thus pass we, in the hush of night,
   Each nerve all braced and strong ;
And, with a whirlwind's stunning blow,
   Retrieve our country's wrong.

Look up !   Above the frozen stream
   The sentinels of heaven —
The pure, serene, and holy stars—.
   Keep watch and ward at even.

And thus the tranquil light of Trust
   No chilling doubt may hide ;
Like pencilled ray from upper dome,
   It travels by our side.

Defeat but rallies to our aid
   The noble and the true ;
Defeat the hero's heart has made
   But thrill with hope anew.

No sleep to-night !   Our Christmas-eve,
   'Mid cold, is bravely passed.
Wait but the first gray streak of dawn,
   And then the bugle-blast

Upon the Hessians' startled host
  Will break, with wizard spell,
And we, with guarded captive-train,
  Hold joyous festival.

THE OMEN AT PRINCETON.

The frame in which the portrait of King George was suspended was subsequently honored with the likeness of Washington. The canvas on which the features of royalty were depicted was shot away by a cannon-ball at the battle of Princeton.

ROUND the College blazed the cannon,
  And the portals, like a leaf,
Quivered at the thundering volley,
  Ordered by the rebel chief;
High above the tide of battle,
  Surging as a lava wave,
Floated Freedom's glorious pennon,
  Borne aloft by spirits brave.

Wheel the ordnance to the centre
  (Thus the voice its burden sent),
Sweep the door so barricaded,
  Give the foe stern punishment;
Enfilade the hall of science,
  Storm them in their fine retreat;
Death, amid the field of letters,
  May pour lustre on defeat.

Flew the balls where sons of Wisdom
  Peacefully their classic lore
Oft had conned, and inly pondered,
  Thus augmenting learning's store.
Mars had now displaced Minerva,
  And his brazen corselet rang,
And his bow-string, old and trusty,
  Gave its own sonorous twang.

In a recess hung a portrait,
  Picturing King George's face,
And its brow was peering proudly
  Now within that leaguered place ;
But a ball came whizzing sternly,
  Like a tongue of Etna flame,
And, as if by Heaven directed,
  Cut the canvas from the frame.

There the gilded wood was hanging,
  Like a poor, deserted throne,
From whose seat a king departing
  Left its tinsel gauds alone.
Swift, almost, as flash in summer,
  Swift as bird upon the wing,
All the labor of the artist,
  Like a flake, was vanishing.

What an omen, sure and precious !
  What a lesson, taught of God !

32

Royalty was soon to perish,—
    Perish at the people's nod.
Soon did Freedom, blest protector,
    She whom despots could not tame,
Sunder all our country's fetters,
    Cut like canvas from the frame.

SURRENDER OF BURGOYNE.

A MORNING in October; the forest-leaves were
    brown;
The trees their leafy honors were showering freely
    down,
The river danced, as sunlight came trembling to
    its breast,
And autumn in its garniture was beautifully drest.
Out of their camp an army marched, with solemn
    tread and slow;
The trumpeters were silent now, no note had they
    to blow;
St. George's banner drooped in dust as 'twould
    not rise again,
And England's chivalry was dim on Saratoga's
    plain.

A morning in October; the sky was all aglow,
And so was Gates, the rebel chief, with rapture's
    overflow.

3   33

To Canada Burgoyne the bold can never force his
way,
And now his stern six thousand are doomed to
yield the day.
Sir Henry Clinton hastens not with reinforcement strong ;
For up the Hudson, with his troops, his ships are
borne along.
St. George's banner droops in dust, as 'twould
not rise again,
And England's chivalry is dim on Saratoga's
plain.

A morning in October ; ho ! Gates, thou art master
here !
Thy mandate ringeth potently upon the foeman's
ear.
See how, upon the river's verge, their shining
arms they pile,
While Nature seems to give thee congratulation's
smile.
How Washington will triumph, when to his ear
has sped
The news, which soon its rapture within his heart
shall shed ;
The news which proves that royal pride is vanquished now and slain ;
That England's chivalry is dim on Saratoga's
plain.

When from Ticonderoga thy forces marched in
glee,
Ah, didst thou think, Burgoyne the bold, defeat
awaited thee?
When to Fort Edward fled in haste our panic-
stricken band,
Say, didst thou not toward them point thy own
deriding hand?
But Fate has turned the fickle tide, and now our
eagle's eye
Drinks in, unchecked, the splendors of a pro-
pitious sky.
Well may thy gorgeous banner droop as 'twould
not rise again,
For England's chivalry is dim on Saratoga's
plain.

Six thousand strong,—six thousand strong,—ah!
ye are now but weak ;
No flush comes o'er your face to-day, your bold
success to speak.
Pile up the arms ; ye fight no more ; the God of
hosts decrees
That all your power shall shake and fall, like
autumn leaves from trees.
Learn, learn the truth,—that Freedom's cause is
still the cause of Heaven ;
Know, for a surety, all our chains, though massive, shall be riven.

35

Go back to royalty, Burgoyne, nor be thy mes-
   sage vain,
And may thy sovereign wisdom learn from Saratoga's plain.

RETREAT FROM BARREN HILL.

A MORN in May, and Howe and Grant held con-
   verse deep and low,
Concerting how they might dislodge their strongly
   posted foe ;
East of the Schuylkill's stream, they knew, the
   firm intrenchment lay,
Where Lafayette, the chieftain, stood, in all his
   bright array.
And thus Lord Howe began, in tones as measured
   and as stern
As ever mark the lion-hearts on battle-fields who
   learn :

"The boy of France has arrogance within his
   panting breast,
Since in the rebel cause his king companionship
   experts,
As if the Bourbon, by his pen, proclaiming traitors
   free,

Could snatch a falling land from what must be its
    destiny ;
As if the Fleur-de-lis had strength within our
    breath to thrive,
And by its blooming petals could a scentless shrub
    revive.
In commerce and alliance an ancient Christian
    crown,
Forgetful of its dignity, has stooped to rebels
    down ;
And joy was in that rebel camp, and salvos shook
    the ground,
And eloquence proclaimed the news with syllables
    profound.
Why, Grant, it stings me to the quick to see the
    dastard brood
Thus revelling like buccaneers within the wild
    greenwood,
As if the Lion's crest had fallen, as if our sinewy arm
Was by a treaty paralyzed and robbed of vigor
    warm.
Go, Grant, and take thy chosen force, and march
    to Barren Hill,
And let the cannon tell the tale that Britons we
    are still ;
Surprise the boy of France at once, and by thy
    victor word
Strip from him all his chosen host as plumage
    from the bird ;

Silence the battery,—shall he dare to post himself
    so high,
While quartered yet in Valley Forge the menial
    forces lie?
Forward! your very chargers prance, and this be
    still your tone,—
'Down with the rebel foe and France! Saint
    George and Albion!'"

*   *   *   *   *   *   *

Militia on the lookout! deserted is your post;
Grant will effect his purpose, and Lafayette be
    lost.
Militia on the lookout! how faithless to your
    trust!
Your country's banner-fold, to-day, through you
    may trail in dust.
Down on your forces, like a hawk, he makes a
    circling sweep,—
He, Grant the Briton, who your cause in infamy
    would steep.
Ah! Lafayette, 'twill tax your skill to draw your
    forces off;
Mature your measures quickly now, or be the
    foeman's scoff;
In fertile policy to-day be all thy wisdom shown,
And tho' a boy in years, thou shalt in acts a man
    be known.
Draw off thy forces to the camp, and never lose a
    man;

Stamp conquest even on retreat, and march with
　　rear and van ;
Elude the snare with wary heart, and when the
　　net is thrown,
Theirs be the blank astonishment to find the prey
　　is gone.

*　　*　　*　　*　　*　　*　　*

Joy in the camp at Valley Forge,—two thousand
　　chosen men
Are piping out the roundelay, like maidens in a
　　glen ;
And Barren Hill becomes a name potential in its
　　spell ;
For there the gallant Lafayette performed the
　　hero well,
And Grant went back to Howe chagrined, with
　　drooping rear and van,
To whimper how, at Barren Hill, the *boy had foiled
the man.*

THE VICTORY AT MONMOUTH.

" HOLD them in check,—that British host,
　　Till I bring up the van ;
And, Lee, whatever be the cost,
　　Be sure to play the man.

Clinton at Monmouth halts to-day,
  All waiting for our blow,
And what will Howe, his chieftain, say
  Upon his overthrow?
Remember Valley Forge, and stir
  Thy every pulse to life;
Remember Valley Forge, nor err,
  When once begins the strife.
Decision, prudence, zeal, be thine,
  A will of iron power;
Each element of force combine,
  And grasp the favoring hour.
I lean on thee : my bursting heart
  Has had its days of gloom;
But still I hoped a *rill* would start,—
  A *flower* in sunlight bloom.
Hold them in check, that British host,
  Till I bring up the van;
And, Lee, whatever be the cost,
  Be sure to play the man.''

Time sped, and Washington advanced
  To grapple with the strong,
His warrior spirit all entranced
  With notes of victor-song,—
When on, in full retreat, came Lee,
  With charger wet with foam.
Why did his reinforcement flee?
  Why did he not strike home?

" Go back, oh, recreant, turn the tide,
  Ere we be swept away ;
Go back, nor let my soul deride
  To see the great decay."

Stung to the quick, he spurred his steed,
  And brought his troops to bear.
Alas ! the tempest-shaken reed
  Defeat again must share ;
Thus driven back afresh, there came
  That thunderbolt of war,
And Washington, like Etna flame,
  Became the guiding star.
Give way !—his cannons blaze in might ;
  Give way !—his sword is strong ;
Or ere the shades of coming night
  Will be avenged the wrong.
To Sandy Hook, that night, withdrew
  The shattered British host.
Clinton the rebels' courage knew,
  And Monmouth was our boast.

MIDDLEBROOK.

In the autumn succeeding the battle of Monmouth, Washington took up his winter quarters in huts which he had caused to be constructed at Middlebrook, in New Jersey.

THE lowly huts of Middlebrook,
    Which sheltered from the storm
Those who from God their lesson took,
    Nor bowed to human form,—
What glory gathers round the spot,
    Like aureola gleam !
And passing time eclipses not
    Of light that radiant stream.

The crowded huts of Middlebrook !
    Our Roman sires were there,
Who on the future dared to look,
    And knew not to despair.
'Mid autumn's foliage sere and dead,
    'Mid winter's snow and blast,
Hope, like the Eastern palm-tree, spread,
    And flourished to the last.

Sequestered huts of Middlebrook !
    The nation's heart beat high,
When Clinton fled to Sandy Hook,
    And '' Monmouth !'' was our cry.

And they who played the hero then
  *Have passed to dust away,
And the log-built homes of truest men
  Have yielded to decay.

But hopes that rose at Middlebrook,
  And stern resolves, that there
Once murmured in a lowly nook,
  Are passing everywhere ;
They speed around the earth, and shake
  The crumbling thrones of kings ;
And despots start, to cringe and quake,
  And feel like guilty things.

Oh ! sainted hearts at Middlebrook,
  Your mission was sublime ;
The cause you never once forsook
  Is bounded by no clime.
That cause,—the cause of truth and right,—
  Omnipotent as God,
Is destined to go forth and smite
  With more than Aaron's rod.

Thrice holy spot of Middlebrook !
  A Mecca to the heart,
As on thy lowly huts we look,
  A Delphian shrine thou art,

And in the camp-fire's ruddy gleam,
    Which fancy lights anew,
There bursts a holier, heavenlier beam
    Than e'er Prometheus drew.

The lowly huts of Middlebrook !
    Our fathers rested there ;
And green forever be the nook,
    And pure that Jersey air ;
And may the pillar and the cloud
    That went before their host
Still rear its canopy of flame,
    Nor by their sons be lost.

WYOMING.

  Wyoming, in Pennsylvania, was a flourishing settlement, containing about one thousand inhabitants. The Tories of the neighborhood, uniting with the hostile Indians, in the summer of 1778, massacred a large number and laid waste the country. This atrocity gave a sterner aspect to the subsequent character of the war.—*Frost's History*, page 254.

A DEMON yell, the flash of steel, and massacre
    complete ;
All hope shut out, one rayless void, no refuge, no
    retreat ;

The matron at her peaceful hearth, the maiden
    'mid her glee,
The yeoman at his noonday meal beneath the
    homestead tree,
The grandame by whose side in joy her daughter's
    children played,
And nosegays from the perfumed flowers with
    agile fingers made ;—
All sunk in death when treachery performed its
    function base,
And the plumed savage swept in wrath through
    Nature's loveliest place.

Wyoming vale ! how beautiful upon that summer
    morn,
Ere rapine's cry upon the gale so terribly was
    borne,
Ere Tories urged a fiendish tribe to mar the quiet
    scene,
Where Peace on conscious Innocence all trustingly
    could lean !
Wyoming vale ! how beautiful, till serpents trail'd
    along,
And brothers of a common blood concerted cruel
    wrong ;
Till Loyalists with double heart could stimulate a
    foe,
Who, once in carnage but embarked, no mild re-
    lenting know !

From farm to farm the tidings spread, and terror-
    stricken men
Rush forth in haste, to never see the lowly hearth
    again,
With food and raiment left untouched, and money's
    garnered store,
The surging flame behind, alas! and stern, stern
    want before.
Base, base the hearts that plotted deep! Can Sus-
    quehanna's flood
Wash out from candid page of truth that chron-
    icle of blood?
No!—treachery so marked as this, on iron tablet
    traced,
Can never, by the lapse of time, be softened or
    effaced.

Advance, ye Continental troops! drive off the
    savage foe,
And bid Wyoming's vale again its cultured beauty
    show.
Hide, hide yourselves, ye Tory band; revenge no
    longer sleeps,
And Justice puts the helmet on when suffering
    Goodness weeps;
In sternest fray the thought will come how inno-
    cence has bled;
How through the air to lowly hearts the barbed
    arrows sped.

Then ! then ! ye Continental troops, with British
    foe in sight,
Recall Wyoming's peaceful vale and all the past
    requite.

PUTNAM'S LEAP.

PUT rowels to thy steed, and sweep
    The hundred steps of stone,
And Fame shall canonize thy leap,
    And make thy deed our own.

Thy outpost has been visited,
    Thy men are few but tried,
And if to field of action led,
    Would be their leader's pride.

Tryon approaches—foot and horse !
    Now plant the cannon high !
And bid the hail, with whirlwind force,
    From each old field-piece fly.

Retard their progress,—bid thy men
    To yonder swamp withdraw ;
Put rowels to thy steed—and then,
    Escape the vulture's maw.

The precipice is near the church,
　With hundred steps of stone,—
Leave Tryon gaping in the lurch,
　To find the bird has flown.

One plunge—and he has cleared the steep,
　While British bullets shower.
Ah, Albion's cavalry ! that leap
　Has far eclipsed your power.

Onward, ye brave dragoons ! pursue !
　Let not the steep appall ;
One rebel in his Buff and Blue
　Must not outstrip you all.

What ! fifteen hundred foiled by one,
　Who scours the plain below?
On, Tryon ! face the risk he run,
　Or laurel-wreath forego.

To Stamford hastens Putnam now
　His band to reinforce,
And with cool nerve and honest brow
　Starts fresh upon the course.

He faces quick about,—pursues
　Tryon's returning host,
Happy, when he the day reviews,
　To count no moment lost.

Intrepid spirit ! how sublime
  Thy thrice adventurous deed !
And yet shall live through coming time
  The rider and his steed !

STONY POINT.

On the 15th of July, 1779, Washington despatched
General Wayne to Stony Point to dislodge the British
garrison. The fort was carried by storm, five hundred
and forty-eight being taken prisoners and sixty-three
killed, while the ordnance, standard, and military stores
fell into the possession of the conquerors.—*Frost's History*, **page 258.**

OF all the brave heroes who figured in arms,
  In garrison warfare or fray on the plain,
Whose steel of pure azure was circled with charms,
  Who, who could compete with mad Anthony
    Wayne?

He rushed to the charge like a bird on the wing,
  As sweeps the Euroclydon over the main,
And as the clear sound of his muskets would ring,
  His men gave a cheer for old Anthony Wayne.

'Twas a midsummer day, and our Washington
    said.
  "Yon Stony Point fortress I think we might
    gain."

4   49

" I will fight in the sun, or if not, in the shade,
   But take it I must," vowed our Anthony
     Wayne.

" Its stores and its ordnance we must secure,
   Its standards which wave from the battlement
     tall ;
Our bayonets' charge will be solid and sure,
   Like bees we will pour through the breach in
     the wall.

" Six hundred are there in a bulwark of pride,
   And the juice of the grape floweth free in their
     bowl,
And the downfall of rebels they pledge in the
     tide,
   By the ashes of Warren ! I'll capture the
     whole.

" Virginia laments for her Suffolk in dust,
   East Haven is gone by the torch of the foe,
And Fairfield and Norwalk have sated their lust,
   And the sons of Connecticut fall by the blow.

" By those hearths which are desolate, mothers are
     pale,
   And the tear-drops of beauty distill as the rain,
But the cry of Revenge ! shall be borne on the
     gale,
   And he who will swell it is Anthony Wayne."

'Twas musket to musket the rampart was scaled,
  And men were contending with sinews of steel,
And nerves that were strung for the contest now
      failed,
    While foemen at last had to falter and reel.

Dislodged was the enemy ; ordnance and store
    Changed hands in the struggle, and fell to his
      lot.
A wound from the action the conqueror bore,
    But reckless was he of the blade or the shot.

For sixty had swelled the stern list of their dead,
    And five times an hundred were led in his train.
O'er Stony Point fortress a halo was shed,—
    That halo was kindled by Anthony Wayne.

THE MUSCOVY DRAKE.

Mrs. Sabina Elliott, a Southern lady, having beheld
the activity of an English officer in plundering her
poultry-yard, and finding an old Muscovy drake which
had escaped the search, ordered her servant to follow on
horseback and deliver the fowl to the officer with her
compliments, concluding that in his hurry he had left it
by mistake.—*Grimshaw's History*, page 179.

He ranged with glee among chickens and geese,
For their rebel owner he longed to fleece,
    Though she was a Southern fair ;

Her raven curls and her hazel eye
Had failed to arouse his chivalry,
  So the poultry-house was bare.

She could not censure the gallant act,
For the towns of rebels were often sacked,
  And rebel hen-coops too ;
And to make the feathery legion tramp,
Like trembling prisoners from their camp,
  Would his martial zeal renew.

A dainty stomach the soldier had,
And a piece of the breast would not taste bad
  With a little generous Hock ;
The leg of the goose and the turkey-wing,
With some onion-sauce, would be just the thing,
  Epicurus would own the stock.

Saint George's men never stooped to care ;
Some quarter was bound to supply the fare,
  And that of the choicest brand ;
They drove off cows and they captured sheep,
And among the poultry how clean a sweep
  They made with an outstretched hand !

But, officer bold, you were not awake
When you slighted that old Muscovy drake,
  And paid no respect to age.
Did you think for carving 'twould be too tough ?
Your sword-blade is certainly keen enough
  Dissection's war to wage.

52

Ah ! Mistress Sabina Elliott
" A rod in pickle" has surely got
   For the gallant cavalier.
" Haste, Thomas, and saddle the horse," says she,
" And take the old drake for company,
   And straight for his honor steer."

Off galloped the steed with flowing mane,
And Thomas was Gilpin o'er again,
   While scudding before the wind ;
He gained on the man in the red cloth gay,
And his Missus had taught him what to say,
   And 'twas easy the words to find.

" Respects to Gineral, but by mistake
He left in de rear de Muscovy drake,
   But carried away de chicken ;
My Missus desires her compliments,
And here I give 'em to all intents,
   And success attend de pickin'."

MARION'S DINNER.

A British officer, sent to negotiate an exchange of prisoners, was conducted into Marion's encampment. There the scene took place which is here commemorated. The young officer was so deeply affected by the sentiments of Marion that he subsequently resigned his commission and retired from the British service.—*Grimshaw's History*, page 163.

THEY sat on the trunk of a fallen pine,
    And their plate was a piece of bark,
And the sweet potatoes were superfine,
    Though bearing the embers' mark ;
But Tom, with the sleeve of his cotton shirt,
    The embers had brushed away,
And then to the brook, with a step alert,
    He hied on that gala day.

The British officer tried to eat,
    But his nerves were out of tune,
And, ill at ease on his novel seat,
    While absent both knife and spoon,
Said he :—" You give me but Lenten fare ;
    Is the table thus always slim ?
Perhaps with a Briton you will not share
    The cup with a flowing brim ?"

Then Marion put his potato down
    On the homely plate of bark,— •
He had to smile, for he could not frown,
    While gay as the morning lark,—
"'Tis a royal feast I provide to-day ;
    Upon roots we rebels dine ;
And in Freedom's service we draw no pay ;
    Is that code of ethics thine ?"

Then, with flashing eye and with heaving breast,
   He looked to the azure sky,
And, said he, with a firm, undaunted crest,
   "Our trust is in God on high.
The hard, hard ground is a downy bed,
   And hunger its fang foregoes,
And noble and firm is the soldier's tread
   In the face of his country's foes."

The officer gazed on that princely brow,
   Where valor and genius shone,
And upon that fallen pine his vow
   Went up to his Maker's throne :
" I will draw no sword against men like these ;
   It would drop from a nerveless hand,
And the very blood in my heart would freeze
   If I faced such a Spartan band."

From Marion's camp, with a saddened mien,
   He hastened with awe away ;
The sons of Anak his eyes had seen,
   And a giant race were they.
No more on the tented field was he,
   And rich was the truth he learned,
That men who could starve for Liberty
   Can neither be crushed nor spurned.

OLD CONTINENTAL PAPER.

The paper currency issued by Congress first appeared in the latter part of 1775. Its depreciation was gradual. In a few places it continued to circulate for the first four months of 1781. The author, when a boy, used to gaze with deep interest at one of these old notes in his father's possession, and the reflections subjoined do but embody his youthful emotions at the time.

TO THE MEMORY OF ROBERT MORRIS, FINANCIER OF
A STRUGGLING COUNTRY.

OLD Continental paper ! the saffron hue of time
Has stolen o'er thy texture, once clear when in its
     prime ;
The figures on thy face, once fresh, look patri-
     archal sadly,
And note-engravers might impugn thy execution
     madly ;
But yellow and antique as thou to other eyes may'st
     be,
Old Continental paper ! thou hast mystic charms
     for me :
I take thee in my hand, and mark the names
     which gave thee worth,
When thou, a goodly pioneer, didst hail a nation's
     birth ;
And that dear, old-fashioned Congress, a Spartan
     band, I see,

Declaring, with united breath, that God had made
    them free ;
The form of Patrick Henry looms up in giant phase,
And the very smile of hope I catch which o'er
    his features plays,
As, flinging upward to the heavens his sinewy
    arm, he cries,
"Up, and smite off your fetters ! Rise, like the
    ocean, rise !"
Old Continental paper ! thou pealest in my ear
The battle-cry of Bunker Hill when scarlet coats
    drew near.
I view the face of Warren in thy rough-shaped
    letters, plain,
And as Freedom's proto-martyr, I note him with
    the slain.
The snows of Valley Forge, anon, are crimsoning
    in my view,
Where blood had marked the footprints of the
    loyal and the true,
And the Leader rests his pensive brow upon his
    hands at night,
For, through the thickening shadows, Hope casts
    but taper light.
Old Continental paper ! the name of Brandywine,
Of Monmouth, and of Princeton too, are braided
    into thine,
And Yorktown, where the grounded arms and
    folded banner said :

"The king that sought the young child's life—
    fair Freedom's life—is dead !
Dead in his influence to harm, dead in his potent
    sway,
Thrice dead in his design to wrench your chartered
    rights away !"
Yorktown ! where scarlet coats defiled before the
    Buff and Blue
In a silence to that lengthened line as strange as it
    was true !
Old Continental paper ! the letters on thy face
Call from their graves the Mothers of that more
    than Spartan race,—
Women who melted into balls the good old leaden
    sashes,
And filled the knapsacks with the stuff to deal out
    rebel gashes ;
Women who made the *homespun*, and put it on
    their sons,
And bade their husbands say farewell to wife and
    little ones ;
Women who gave the shield and said, not in a
    measured sonnet,
But in stern Saxon syllables, "Come *with* it, or
    upon it !"
Old Continental paper ! we have grown a mighty
    size,
And we begin to "*calculate*" that we are rich and
    wise.

Labor is at his wheel in peace, and Science on her
     chair,
And the flag which guards our commerce is float-
     ing everywhere ;
The golden harvest waveth, and the reaper singeth
     free,
And all these blessed issues we associate with *thee.*
Far to the West there floweth a vast commingled
     tide,
As when from Egypt marched the Jews, unfettered
     and in pride ;
They caught the guiding ray of hope when far
     across the main,
And can they in their prison-house another hour
     remain ?
No ; o'er the surging billows to the regions of the
     West,
Where peace and plenty stretch their arms, be-
     guiling them to rest.
No ; gardens must be planted where rise those
     forests dim ;
Their sounding aisles shall echo to childhood's
     freedom hymn ;
These thronging bands, whose axes' ring betokens
     progress yet,
Who in our land the bitter ills of serfdom's lot
     forget ;
These moving myriads pressing on to mingle with
     the free,

Are linked with thy old yellow page, oh, how un-
    dyingly !

Let beauteous issues of the Bank invite us to
    ignore

The history of that olden Note which toddled on
    before,—

That olden Note, upon whose faith our fathers
    fought and won,

Bequeathing better currency when the toilsome
    work was done !

No graver's art can execute a bill with half the
    charm

Which bids those faded figures assume a mantle
    warm,

For all our past achievements bright, and all we
    hope to be,

Are of thyself a living part,—*are warp and woof*
    with thee !

FLAMBOROUGH HEAD.

On the 23d of September, 1779, took place that most
memorable encounter between the " Bon Homme Richard," under the command of Paul Jones, and the British
frigate " Serapis," of forty-four guns. The action took

place off Flamborough Head ; the moon was shining ;
and the action, which lasted four hours, was witnessed
by thousands of interested spectators.

MOONLIGHT was on the wave ; September's eve
Was calm and beautiful ; the swell and heave
Of ocean's billow came upon the ear
Like music mellowed in an upper sphere.
The line of coast was throng'd, for hearts will
      leap
When Mars comes down to reign upon the deep.
That thunderbolt of war, intrepid Paul,
With conquest ever at his wizard call,
In sight of Scotia's port, the town of Leith,
Had won in honest strife the warrior's wreath.
The "Pallas" and the "Vengeance" there awoke
Their slumbering guns, that tones emphatic spoke.
Now the "Serapis" would he capture here,
Where the bold headland rises true and clear.
But late, with crew select, she sailed in pride ;
No ship more buoyant ever clove the tide.
The "Bon Homme Richard" dares not to com-
      pete
With the proud frigate, jewel of the fleet.
But in her captain's iron will her trust ;
If Paul say "Conquer," conquer then he must.
If in his might he bid the broadside tell,
Each plank of British oak shall feel the spell,
The mizzen tremble like an autumn leaf,
And the hull shake as harvest's nodding sheaf.

See ! the " Serapis" breaks the silence.   See !
That raking broadside, Paul, was meant for thee.
Hark ! how the shout from Flamborough arose,
While the full moon inspirited the foes.
But wait till o' er the tide the galling shower
Shall open seams within thy sides of power.
Stern, full, relentless, every rebel ball, .
Like Vulcan's bolt, with vengeful strength must
     fall.
Now from the " Bon Homme" comes the quick
     reply,
And lights the headland and the autumn sky ;
And on the coast deep feelings ebb and flow.
The cheek in pallor, or the heart's stern throe,
Attest the interest of the spell-bound throng,
And how emotion's current hastes along.
Look up ! the British bowsprit thou canst hold,
For o' er thy poop it comes. Rouse, warrior bold !
Seize, seize the ropes which from that bowsprit
     hang
And make them fast.   Ah ! how the welkin rang
When, swinging round, alongside thus she lay !
And when with heightening ardor raged the fray,
The bow of one close to its neighbor's stern,
The cordage flames, the seasoned timbers burn,
Commingled prayers and imprecations rise ;·
The foeman's mainmast totters, then it lies,
Like the tall giant, when he bent the head,
And awed Philistia knew her champion dead.

Strike, strike your colors ! Soon the midnight bell
Will sound for many a tar its solemn knell.
The " Bon Homme Richard" soon must sink like
    lead,
When all her wounded on your deck are spread.
But Freedom's cause shall never thus be merged
While her bold claim by iron hearts is urged.
Let but such men as he whose stentor tone
Made every sailor its bewitchment own ;
Let but such men as Paul the flag defend,
And Britain's monarch may his raiment rend,
And Flamborough head be but the exponent
    stern
Of what we rebels teach, and what the Crown must
    learn.

THE SOLILOQUY OF ARNOLD.

When he was invested with the command of West
Point by Washington, General Arnold entered into a
secret correspondence with Sir Henry Clinton, and
agreed that he would make a disposition of his forces
which would enable the British general to surprise the
post under such circumstances that the garrison must
either lay down their arms or be cut to pieces.

THE plan is fixed. I fluctuate no more
Betwixt despair and hope. As leaves the shore
The hardy mariner, though adverse fate
May merge his bark, or cast him desolate

Upon a savage coast, so, wrought at last
Up to a frenzied purpose, I have passed
The Rubicon.   Farewell, my old renown !
Here I breathe mildew on my warrior crown ;
Here honor parts from me, and base deceit
Steps to the usurper's throne.   I cannot meet
The withering censure of the rebel band,
And therefore to the strong I yield this heart and
    hand.

What else befits me?   I have misapplied
The nation's funds, and ever gratified
Each vaulting wish, tho' Justice wept the deed ;
And here, beneath the load of pressing need,
I must have gold.   How else the clamorous cry
Of creditors appease, and satisfy
Demands which haunt me more than dreams of
    blood,
And claims which chill more than Canadian flood?
Stay?   My accounts betray the swindler's mark.
Go? and my path, though smooth, like Tartarus
    is dark.

These rocky ridges, how they shelve on high,
Each a stern sentinel in majesty.
Yes, 'tis your own Gibraltar, —Washington.
And must the stronghold of his hope be won?
Won?   Twenty thousand scarcely could invest
That sure defence, which o'er the river's breast

Casts a gigantic shadow ; but my plan
Dispenses with the formidable van,
And Clinton may my garrison surprise,
With few sulphureous clouds to blot these azure
    skies.

And yet a pang comes over me.　I see
Myself at Saratoga ; full and free
Goes up the peal of noble-hearted men.
Among the wounded am I numbered then ;
And my outgushing feelings cling to those
Who perilled all to face their country's foes.
Ah ! when that wound a soldier's pride increased,
And gratulation scarce its pæan ceased,
I thought not then, O God ! the stamp of shame
Would stand imprinted thus upon my hard-earned
    fame.
Avaunt, compunction ! Conscience, to the wind !
Gold,—gold I need,—gold must Sir Henry find.
A rankling grudge is mine, for why not I
Commander of their forces ?　To the sky
Ever goes up the peal for Washington.
Is he a god, Virginia's favored son ?
Why should the incense fume for evermore ?
Must he my skill, my prowess shadow o'er ?
Ere this autumnal moon has filled its horn,
His honors must be nipp'd, his rising glories
    shorn.

Ah ! he securely rests upon my faith
Securely, when the spectre dims his path.
How unsuspecting has he ever been !
Above the false, the sinister, the mean !
But hold such eulogy ; I will not praise ;
Mine is the task to tarnish all his bays.
West Point, thy rocky ridges seem to say :
Be firm as granite, crown the work to-day,
Blot Saratoga, hearth and home abjure,
André I meet again, the gold I must secure.

THE CAPTURE OF ANDRÉ.

When returning from a conference with Arnold, Major André was intercepted on the 22d of September, near the village of Tarrytown, by three faithful militia soldiers ; John Paulding, Isaac Van Wert, and David Williams, and by the laws of war forfeited his life to a country struggling with an accumulation of disasters. —*Grimshaw's History*, page 169.

THE midnight conference was deep and long,
The plan began with guilt was sealed with wrong.
Between the British and our army's posts,
While slumber settled on the mighty hosts,
Landed in silence from the sloop-of-war
André, of modern chivalry the star,
Young, brave, ingenuous, never more to press
A soldier's couch in hope or happiness.

66

That sloop which bore him owned a fitting name,
The *Vulture*, index of Britannia's shame.
Yes, like *that bird* ye sought but *to devour*,
And glut your vengeance in that gloomy hour.
Arnold was there, and as the time sped by,
Forgot to trace the streakings of the sky,
Till daybreak came, and up the wide expanse
Shot an autumnal sun his rising glance.
The "Vulture," meanwhile, felt the foeman's fire,
And down the stream did prudently retire.
Within our posts conducted, André lay
In dread concealment ; then upon the way
Afresh he started, clad in deep disguise,
Furnished with passports ; and his longing eyes
Strained to the point where Albion's lion crest
Should welcome him to honor and to rest.
Ride on, *John Anderson*,* thy boots contain
The golden documents thy lord would gain.
There, snugly packed, are statements in detail
Which clothe Sir Henry with a coat of mail ;
The key of our Gibraltar is thine own,
And Freedom now must cower beneath the throne.
Safety attends thee still ; the British lines
Are near, yet nearer, and thy planet shines
Auspicious in its mild benignity ;
When, lo ! its disc is darkening.   See, ah ! see

---

* He was thus designated, while Arnold assumed the
name of Gustavus.

Those tall emerging forms.   Detected now,
The diadem will pale upon thy brow.
Question and answer quickly come and go ;
The net its meshes has begun to throw,
And in an iron gripe, whose tightening hold
Relaxes not a particle for gold,
Is André now.   Begin the search, and see
The record deep of man's duplicity.
There Arnold's pen your wondering eyes shall
        meet ;
Haste, bear the packet to your leader's feet.
To you, militiamen, this day is given,
Whether the chain of fate be forged or riven ;
Stern in your honest manhood, take him hence,
And fame will be your bright inheritance ;
On to the quarters of your captain brave,
Secure your prisoner, and your country save.
Paulding, Van Wert, and Williams, noble three !
Your memory greener grows ; and even we
Hold you in grateful reverence, though we sigh
For that poor captured youth thus doomed to die.
Ne'er shall the fact be lost that hearts there are,
Unquelled by *Garter* and unbought by *Star ;*
Whose country's honor far outweighed a crown,
When trembled, to a hair, the scales near Tarry-
        town.

ANDRÉ ON THE EVE OF EXECUTION.

Allusion is made in this lyric to the fact of Washington's deep feeling when he signed the death-warrant; also to the artistic talents of André as a painter and a poet; and, finally, to his memorable saying in reference to the mode of his death, after pleading for the substitution of a nobler one, " It will be but a momentary pang."

THE lilac shall bud and the sweet hawthorn blos-
    som,
  Old Severn shall roll his glad waves to the sea,
But André wlll sleep with the clod on his bosom,
  And the proud dream of glory be darkened for me.
Sir Henry has sued, with a soldier's devotion,
  The scorn to avert and the blow to restrain ;
But give me the cup, and though bitter the
    potion,
  To its dregs, like a hero, the draught I will drain.

To-morrow, with guard, I must march from my
    prison,
  No kindred to cheer me, no comrade to weep ;
By slumber unblest from my pillow I've risen,
  But soon in the tomb how unbroken the sleep !
Dear country ! illumined by actions of glory,
  My blood at thy shrine a libation I pour ;
Let André but live in thy chronicled story,
  And, dying in joy, I petition no more.

In pride I sustained the ordeal of trial,
 Dissemble I would not, concealment I spurned ;
I asked but one boon, it was met with denial,
 Though candor itself said the favor was earned.
I will not upbraid him, the tear fell unbidden,
 When the sweep of his pen darkened nature for
  me,
And I know the full pulse of his mercy was chid-
 den
 When the rope of the culprit was made the de-
  cree.

Oh, son of Virginia ! the well-spring of feeling
 Courses up in thy heart like the tides of the
  main,
And though from the throng thy emotion con-
 cealing,
 A Washington's eye holds its moisture in vain.
Farewell to the hero ! His future shall brighten ;
 I see the clear dawn as I pass to my tomb ;
The burden of care on his spirit will lighten,
 And Hope as his chaplet of amaranth bloom.

When late from the meadows enamelled I bounded,
 And heard the sweet song-bird its melody
  pour,
Ah ! little thought.I, as the war-bugle sounded,
 The music and verdure should greet me no
  more.

The lilac shall bud and the sweet hawthorn blos-
    som,
Old Severn shall roll his glad waves to the sea,
But André shall sleep with the clod on his bosom,
    And the proud dream of glory be darkened for
    me.

My pencil, farewell ! all the tintings of beauty
    The canvas will hold when my heart is at rest.
The art that I cherished, unbending from duty,
    The last I resign, for I prize it the best ;
For, oh, my creations of fancy when tracing,
    The fate of the spy would grow soft by its spell,
But now the stern truth the fair vision is chasing ;
    Art, fondest enchantress, farewell, oh, farewell !

Rise, gild the horizon, last sun of my being ;
    The pang but a moment, eternal the peace.
Home, kindred, and love, like a mist ye are flee-
    ing ;
    One spasm of pain and the conflict will cease.
Oh, England ! illumined by actions of glory,
    My blood at thy shrine a libation I pour ;
Let André but live in thy chronicled story,
    And, dying in joy, I petition no more.

THE BOY HERO OF RAMSOUR'S MILL.

At the battle of Ramsour's Mill, when Captain Falls received a mortal wound and fell, his son, a youth of fourteen, rushed to the body when the man who had shot him was beginning to plunder it, and, regardless of his opponent's strength, snatched up his father's sword and laid him dead at his parent's feet.—*Grimshaw's History.*

THE foeman bent, with lucre-loving heart,
   Above the rebel's scarcely breathing form,
As if to plunder was the noblest part
   That heroes played in battle's maddening storm.
Oh, what a brand of shame our nature bears,
   When gold the milk of kindness turns to gall,
And Mammon fails to cast aside its cares,
   Though fate should interpose a crimson pall!

Perchance but little spoil would crown the search,
   Some trifling coins, a pencil, or a knife ;
Why should the vulture, sweeping from his
     perch,
   Outrage for these the decencies of life ?
Or why, his task extending, should he claim
   The dripping vestments as a perquisite ?
He thus who gloats on the denuded frame
   Might at the Cross with Roman soldiers sit.

There was an eye that scanned the roving hand ;
  There was a boyish heart that laid aside
Its timid fears, and springing to command,
  Mustered its surges in the boiling tide.
Thoughts of his early life came trooping fast
  Through Memory's portals, and he sat again
Upon a father's knee, when toil was past
  And eve's long shadows stretched across the
    plain.

He felt his loving clasp, his warm breath came,
  Stirring the ringlets on his little head,
And now he saw the plunderer o'er his frame,
  In deep dishonor to the noble dead.
In that brief moment vengeance ruled his soul;
  Like sudden tempest to the charge he swept,
The sword he wielded with a man's control,
  And Mammon's bond-slave back to darkness
    crept.

And yet but fourteen summers he had seen,
  That hero child, who, like Minerva, sprang,
A perfect warrior on the crimson green,
  Prepared Bellona's massive bow to twang.
He, whose dear, gentle spirit would recoil
  At pain inflicted on the creeping worm,
Could sternly guard his own invaded soil,
  And be for justice as Gibraltar firm.

There is a depth of earnestness in youth,
  A strength of purpose hidden from the sight,
A keen, appreciating sense of Truth,
  A tightening clasp to Honor and to Right.
Let the occasion spring the mine, and then
  Each sleeping germ vitality acquires,
And smooth-cheeked boyhood feels the pulse of
    men,
  And freedom's children emulate their sires.

At Ramsour's Mill the tyrant might despond
  When fledgling rebels made their mark so
    true,
And mothers, as they kissed their children
    fond,
  Bade them do service to the Buff and Blue.
Still may that spirit in our offspring burn,
  Still may the patriot fathers' mantle fall,
That while our ashes rest within the urn
  Freedom may find in them her bold, encircling
    wall.

MARIE ANTOINETTE.

When Louis XVI. of France espoused the cause of the
suffering Americans, he was opposed by the Count de
Vergennes and the Court, but the strong appeal of the

Commissioners, and the very urgent solicitation of his Queen, whom he fondly loved, turned the scale in their favor.

> On the scaffold, reeking yet
>   With her royal husband's blood,
> Kneels Marie Antoinette,
>   Pure, and beautiful, and good,
> 'Mid the strife, and 'mid the din,
>   Calm as summer-breath at even ;
> Ah ! that ice-cold guillotine
>   Does but speed her soul to heaven.
>
> By that scaffold, reeking yet
>   With the blood of Louis brave,
> Love and sorrow to forget,
>   Steadily she scanned the grave,
> And the children of her heart,*
>   And her kingdom's sunny clime,
> She could with them freely part,
>   In a martyr-faith sublime.
>
> Golden is the braided strand,
>   Bright and beauteous is the tie
> Which connects our own dear land
>   With that spirit pure and high.

* She perished on the scaffold in 1793, October 16, with calmness and dignity, nine months after the execution of Louis, leaving the Dauphin and his sister orphans. As an advocate of our country, we love her memory.

To that soft, persuasive tongue,
    When for succor sued the weak,
Sympathetic accents clung,
    All that woman's heart could speak.

O'er the far Atlantic strove
    Freedom, fainting in the fray ;
Must the tempest whelm the dove ?
    Must the Lion rend his prey ?
Will no arm, encased in steel,
    Prop the feeble, staggering band ?
Or, must history reveal
    Heroes' efforts traced in sand ?

" No !" a gentle voice replies,
    And its tones are lofty now ;
See the flashing of her eyes,—
    See the noble, queenly brow !
" No ; our fleet your waves shall grace,
    Bearing thunder as they glide,
And our Fleur-de-lis shall trace
    England on our streamers wide.

" Oh, my husband, bright the gleam
    From the jewels on thy breast,
And as childhood's pleasant dream,
    Calm will be thy evening's rest
When thy pen, with potent sweep,
    Seals deliverance sure and true,
Faith with Washington to keep,
    Compact thou wilt never rue."

Could such pleading be repelled?
　Could such suit be turned aside?
When Compassion's bosom swelled,
　Must not love be gratified?
Yes, the son of France no more
　Heeded cold, prudential form,
And he pledged his treasured store
　Like a brother in the storm.

Oh, that scaffold where she kneels,
　How our hearts about it cling!
Pity to our bosom steals,
　Sheltered as a sacred thing.
Daughter of a noble line,
　We would not thy name forget,
Green the chaplet we would twine
　Round thy memory, Antoinette!

TARLETON AND THE LADIES.

At a social gathering in Charleston, South Carolina, at which Colonel Tarleton, of the English cavalry, was present as one of the company, some of the ladies complimenting Colonel Washington, he expressed a wish to see him. "Had you looked behind you at the battle of the Cowpens," said a lady, "you might easily have enjoyed that pleasure."—*Grimshaw's History.*

In social festivity passing the hour
　Sat Tarleton, the prince of dragoons,

Now scanning a painting, now smelling a flower,
  Now serving Apollo with tunes ;
The pet of Cornwallis and chivalry's boast,
  The noblest to do and to dare,
At Cowpens he lately had closed with a host,
  And come off rather worse for the wear.

The ladies of Charleston, with radiant face,
  An interlude gave him of joy,
And visions of sabres were banished the place,
  For he felt, in his bliss, like a boy ;
The fire of the demon died out in his heart,
  And harmony gained on his breast,
Till envy compelled him from calmness to start
  At the praise for a rebel expressed.

Colonel Washington's name was the theme of
      their lay,
  Those guardians of merit, the fair, —
His bearing at hearth, and his prowess in fray,
  His manners, his voice, and his air.
Oh, why dost thou wince as the plaudits are rung ?
  Oh, wherefore that cloud of a frown ?
The ladies, you know, have a voluble tongue,
  Which censure may never vote down.

But the prince of dragoons cannot bottle his rage,
  Though graces and fairies are nigh ;
He stoops to a flower, he walks to a cage,
  And thinks, " Like canary am I ;

Surrounded by wires, escape is but vain,
　　But still I will aim to be free ;
And if ever I mix with these ladies again,
　　Then good-by to the sabre for me.

" I often have heard of this hero renowned
　　(At last poured the torrent of ire) ;
It seems that his equal is yet to be found
　　In province, or township, or shire ;
His eulogy comes with an emphasis now,
　　Endorsed by the sweetest of smiles ;
I never have seen him, but, ladies, I vow,
　　It appears worth a journey of miles."

The State of Palmetto was ready with wit,
　　And here was a chance for the girls ;
Of fine Attic salt they would sprinkle a bit,
　　In spite of old England and earls.
Said one, " If behind you a glance you had thrown
　　When beating the Cowpens retreat,*
Colonel Washington then would his visage have
　　　shown,
　　And told you to keep in your seat."

---

　* In the battle of the Cowpens Colonel Washington
made a successful charge upon Colonel Tarleton, who
was cutting down the militia. Colonel W. pursued the
British cavalry for miles, but many of them escaped.
Eight hundred stand of arms, two field-pieces, eighty-five
baggage-wagons, and five hundred prisoners fell into the
hands of the victorious Americans.—*Ramsay's History
of South Carolina.*

THE DEAD IN BATTLE.

SACRED TO THE MEMORY OF THE SOLDIERS OF
OUR ARMY IN THE CONTINENTAL WAR.

SING for the dead in battle ;
   They fell 'mid cannon peal,
The musketry's stern rattle,
   The flash of tempered steel ;
For greener are the hill-tops,
   Which once in youth they trod,
Since those brave hearts were offered
   A holocaust to God.

Where rolls the blue Potomac,
   Where Holyoke's peak doth rise,
And grows the tall palmetto
   Beneath the Southern skies,
From many a scattered homestead
   We see their legions come,
Thrilled by the good old music
   Of Continental drum.

Their golden grain was bending,
   Their sickle was unswung,
No harvest song ascending
   From lusty yeoman's tongue ;
Another field before them
   To enterprise invites,

And ripe, and rich, and beautiful,
   The sheaves of freemen's rights.

Where fought the bold Pulaski,
   And Steuben led the way ;
Where Lafayette was charging,
   On wings of wind were they ;
A body-guard of Spartans
   To Putnam, Gates, and Greene,
Their camp-fires all were kindled,
   Their sentinels were seen.

They asked no rich provision,
   For coarse as was the fare
(And oft 'mid winter's rigor
   Their limbs were cold and bare),
The heart had warm pulsations,
   The arm had sinew free,
And a dream came to their pillows
   Of their children's liberty.

Sing for the dead in battle ;
   They fell 'mid shout and fame,
And musketry's stern rattle
   With death's own anguish came.
But as they passed the portals
   The dew of Hope was shed,
And they blest the cause, immortal,
   For which they freely bled.

Oh, children of the bravest,
   Oh, offspring of the great,
The boon they have bequeathed you
   Preserve inviolate !
From Bunker Hill to Yorktown,
   And thence to Eutaw Springs,
The whole extent is covered
   With more than seraph wings.

The Stripe and Star has floated
   O'er many a league of space,
And States in quick succession
   Have found among us place ;
But resting in their borders,
   And hallowing all the shore,
The spirit of our fathers
   Must linger evermore.

Sing for the dead in battle,
   Sing for the true of heart,
For of our sun-bright heritage
   Are they the choicest part ;
Each pebble is a jewel,
   Where once their footsteps trod,
And where such hearts were offered
   A holocaust to God.

.

GENERAL GREENE AND THE CLAP BOARDS.

After General Nathaniel Greene, in his memorable retreat from Cornwallis, had crossed in succession the rivers Catawba and Yadkin, in North Carolina, he encamped on rising ground beyond the latter stream. Occupying a little frame building himself, with a natural breastwork of rock, he began writing his despatches; but O'Hara, from the other side, commenced a cannonade upon him, which sent the clapboards of the lowly cabin flying in all directions about his head. Such was his composure that he retained his position and completed his despatches.

He sat in a cabin with tranquil mind,
    And a breastwork of rocks before it,
And friend O'Hara was quite inclined
    By a cannonade brisk to gore it;
But Natty Greene was a Quaker raised,
    And the quietness of the spirit
Would not allow him to grow amazed,
    By giving him strength to bear it.

Across Catawba, a rapid stream,
    He had fled with his trusty legion,
And the foeman's sword had a vengeful gleam,
    For it waved in a Tory region;
Across the Yadkin he pushed his way,
    When low was the ebbing water;

But on swept the flags of Cornwallis gay,
   All ready to bathe in slaughter.

But snugly camped on a rising ground,
   With a swollen flood between them,
The rebels laughed at the hail-storm's sound,
   With a breastwork of rock to screen them ;
And the cabin roof, when it caught a rap,
   As it now and then did by snatches,
Gave music to Greene at every tap,
   As he sat and prepared despatches.

Did O'Hara know that the cabin held
   The man who so bravely foiled him?
Did he vow the pea should be fairly shelled
   Before in his rage he boiled him?
Or did he direct a random gun,
   And go by the law of chances ;
Reckless though hundreds miss, if one
   To Nathaniel Greene advances?

The clapboards flew like a frightened flock
   Of birds in a field of clover,
And some of the staff, as they felt the shock,
   Decided that all was over ;
But the wary chief, with his pen in gear,
   Was putting the ink on paper ;
Should he, who had cleared two rivers, fear
   When a shingle cut a caper?

The God of that swollen flood, whose cloud
    Secreted a deluge timely ;
The God of battles, to whom he bowed,
    Could protect his child sublimely ;
Since to Morgan's camp he had turned his face
    When the Cowpens' fray was finished,
That guiding hand he could clearly trace,
    Nor yet was his faith diminished.

There have been hearts who, in danger's hour,
    Have breasted in joy the surges,
And proved that misfortune lost its power
    For such as were Boanerges ;
But surely he who, when clapboards flew,
    Sat writing in calmness under,
By a double claim may the word renew,
    And be known as a Son of Thunder.

KING'S MOUNTAIN.

King's Mountain was an eminence of a circular base.
On this Colonel Ferguson was encamped with the Tories.
Colonels Cleveland, Shelby, Sevier, and Williams led on
to the charge each his own men. Some ascended the
mountain, while others went round its base, in opposite
directions. The action became general. The killed,
wounded, and taken were over eleven hundred. Colonel

Ferguson had previously been training the disaffected young men and enlisting them.—*Ramsay's History of South Carolina.*

WE have him on the mountain now, a lion fierce
    at bay,
Then up, and spread your toils at once, and on to
    the foray ;
Cleveland and Shelby in the van, with Williams in
    the rear,
Flanked by the heart of oak that throbs so sternly
    in Sevier ;
Four rebel knights upon their shields have struck
    a brazen tone,
And given to the waiting winds the spell-word,
    Ferguson !
Around that mountain's rocky base, and up its
    slope of green,
Our rifle-locks will take a hue from heaven's own
    garish sheen.
Upon its apex we must stand, the victors of the
    hour,
And front to front repel the host, whose serried
    columns lower.
King's Mountain ! blot the soaring name ! the
    Tory brood must die ;
While we another title give—the Mount of Lib-
    erty.
Baptized anew, from its broad height the patriot's
    eye shall view,

Through the transforming lens of Hope, a land-
scape bold and new ;
No haze to intercept the beam, whose fairy tint
shall write
Those blessed words " The promised land !" on
every rood in sight.
We have him on the mountain now, he who has
trained our young
To speak of Washington the brave with free and
ribald tongue ;
He who has trailed his serpent length in many a
garden pure,
And by his honeyed speech has made his victim
doubly sure,
His banner with its royal crest, his overtures of guile,
His wild harangue, or flowery tropes, or bland,
seductive smile,
His show of wealth, his promise, too, of guerdons
yet to come,
Have lured our fledglings from their nest, our
children from their home ;
They have been trained by martial rule in fratri-
cidal war, .
Trained on their kin the curse to heap 'neath
Hate's malignant star.
Such tutelage might well become a spirit lost to
shame,
But manhood he has blotted out from his dishon-
ored name.

Injustice finds but sordid means to compass ends
    of wrong,
And truth and goodness prove to it a byword and
    a song.
They march with spirits strung to hope, and round
    the mountain go,
As Hebrew légions once of old surrounded Jericho.
Ho, Ferguson ! the net is laid, the picket-guard
    is vain ;
Rebels can to the mountain press if you refuse the
    plain.
Retreat ye may not, when a belt of galling fire
    surrounds,
And stout Invasion's iron tramp from every
    quarter sounds ;
The thrust and parry of the sword, the hand-to-
    hand foray,
The lips compressed and sullen brow, are all in
    vain to-day.
Schooled in the art of war, and trained to cunning
    and finesse,
Thy tactics, Ferguson the brave, shall never serve
    thee less ;
Above a thousand shall be lost on whom has
    leaned thine arm,
Thy bulwarks must forego their strength, thy
    banner fold its charm.
On, Shelby, to the rescue there ! Press, Williams,
    to his aid !

Look, Cleveland, how the ranks grow thin beneath
    thy trenchant blade ;
And yonder plunges our Sevier amid the heaving
    tide,
Like swimmer, when amid the sea he dashes surge
    aside,
While, with their brows like stiffened cords, the
    standard-bearers leap,
And plant the pennon of the true upon the crim-
    son steep.
Thus Carolina's patriot heart with Washington
    could beat,
And from her borders sounded out " The Loyal-
    ist's Retreat."
No foot of ground to renegades was voted by the
    true,
But all her soil was Holyrood that met the ardent
    view ;
Her pulse was lightning to the touch, when the
    sword she buckled on,
And hunted from his mountain lair the subtle
    Ferguson.

FORT NINETY-SIX.

This important post was commanded by Colonel
Cruger, and defended by five hundred men. General
Greene determined to besiege it in form. He accord-
ingly, on the 25th of May, pushed on his works with

vigor ; but this bright prospect of success was suddenly overclouded by the intelligence that Lord Rawdon, having received reinforcements from Ireland, was hastening to the relief of his countrymen at the head of two thousand men. Greene tried to carry the fort by assault, but was repulsed, and retreated to the northward across the Saluda.

OUR mound was thirty feet in air,
Our riflemen were posted there,
   So strong the vantage ground ;
Saint George and rebels fairly met,
And on the bristling parapet
   We made the bullets sound.

It was the twenty-fifth of May
When freemen caught the reveille
   And sprang before the ditch ;
And Cruger felt how vain his tricks
To keep the fort of Ninety-six
   So close within our reach.

Augusta had surrendered first,
And Lee, who manly hopes had nursed,
   Had proved the Chevalier.
" Push on to Ninety-six," cried Greene,
" To wrench their last defence I mean,
   And keep our border clear."

" Along the Congaree their posts
Have failed to verify the boasts

Which English legions swelled ;
When Marion, from the everglades,
Put lightning in his rusty blades,
  The vaunting heart has quailed."

Then merrily the ground we broke,
And music lingered in the stroke,
  And pushed our works with form;
For hands untrained were quick to learn,
And brows were fixed and looks were stern,
  Precursive of the storm.

"They'll beat a parley, yet," said Greene,
"Savannah's waters with their sheen
  Shall dance in double joy,
For on the crested parapet
Our rifle-balls are ringing yet,
  And powder is our toy."

"But Rawdon comes to reinforce !"
Alas ! like note of raven hoarse
  Fell the announcement dire ;
From Ireland he has drawn the band,
And his may prove a wizard wand
  To intermit our fire.

Hard is it for the gallant ship
To find her solid cable slip
  When she would grasp the shore.

Hard was it at the Isthmian race
For combatant to yield his place
    And sink to run no more.

Thus reaching to the golden fruit,
We had to yield,—in hot pursuit
    Pressed Rawdon on our men.
"Wheel, and retreat," the words of gloom,
The flower is frosted in its bloom,
    It cannot scent the glen.

But when the timid said to Greene,
"In old Virginia be thou seen,
    And be from care exempt,"
He cried with words of proud disdain,
"Our Carolina I will gain
    Or die in the attempt!"

THE HEIGHTS ABOVE SANTEE.

To Orangeburg retreats
    Lord Rawdon with his band,
And Colonel Cruger meets,
    With forces at command.
And now its fold invites
    That banner of the free,
Where it mantles on the heights,
    On the heights above Santee.

The scouting-parties haste,
　With Sumter in the van,
And Marion firmly braced,
　To play again the man.
"From Charleston keep them back,
　Lest stronger grown than we,
They should evade our track
　From the heights above Santee."

"What is the news?" said Greene,
　"My scouting-parties brave?"
"The British flag is seen
　By Congaree's blue wave."
"Then onward, hearts of oak,
　Such is the sure decree,
If they invite the stroke
　From the heights above Santee."

Forth pealed the clarion note,
　The bold battalion goes,
The trumpet's brazen throat
　Anticipates the blows.
But Rawdon still retreats,
　With feeble heart and knee,
For a drum behind him beats
　From the heights above Santee.

At Eutaw Springs they halt,
　Like panting stag at bay ;
Ah ! yonder azure vault
　Shall blush ere close of day.

93

For the red cloud of war
   The zenith soon must see,
Its masses roll from far,
   From the heights above Santee.

" Regain the State you love,
   Old Carolina brave !
They who for lordship strove
   May measure here a grave !
Strike for your leader, Greene,
   A thunderbolt is he,
Whose camp-fires late were seen
   On the heights above Santee."

The musket gives the ball,
   The clashing sword-blade rings,
And hundreds fighting fall
   In the fray at Eutaw Springs;
To Charleston fled the rest,
   Like phantoms o'er the lea,
To one small section prest,
   From the heights above Santee.

Give to the patriot chief
   The captured standard now,*
And trace in bold relief
   Upon the gold his brow.

---

*After the battle of Eutaw Springs, where the English,
under Lord Rawdon, lost eleven hundred in killed and

The locust horde he swept
From mainland to the sea,
When to the vale he stept
From the heights above Santee !

COLONEL HAYNE.

When Colonel Hayne, at the capitulation of Charleston, surrendered himself to the British, he was told that he must either take the oath of allegiance to his Britannic Majesty or submit to close confinement. He took the oath, assured that he would not be called upon at any future period to take up arms against his country. This, however, was enjoined subsequently, and, refusing to do it, he took up arms for liberty, was taken prisoner, and executed.

THEY told me, if the oath I took to Albion's lord
and king,
I need not yet against my land a hostile weapon
bring ;
They told me, and I dreamed that faith in camps
could yet remain,

prisoners, and the Americans five hundred, including sixty officers, the enemy left the interior State of South Carolina and took shelter in Charleston. A gold medal and a captured British standard were bestowed by the Continental Congress, on this memorable occasion, upon General Nathaniel Greene. He had marched from the heights above Santee and pursued the forces of Cruger and Rawdon till they halted for action.

95

That on my hands there need not rest one fratri-
cidal stain.
Now am I summoned to a task my inmost heart
which thrills,
To whirl the flaming brand of war upon my native
hills ;
To send the steely truncheon bright against the
breasts of men
Who long have pledged to Freedom's cause the
willing sword and pen.
Oh, deep enough the stigma now, to think the
oath I took,
And the dear cause, the mighty cause, in evil hour
forsook.
Better within the prisoner's cage be cooped as
fettered bird
Than breathe an atmosphere of joy and feel that
I have erred ;
Better within the murky ship, which looms above
the bay,
Than look on scornful brows and think, 'tis fearful
to betray.
Oh, from the hour when virtue drooped my heart
has been a cell,
Where stern Remorse, and Grief, and Shame
have come in turn to dwell.
Why not adhere to wounded Right ? Why pros-
trate Right in dust ?

Why think the recreant was secure when on the
　　lava crust?
The lava crust of policy, how brittle in its
　　form,
And glowing just beneath the shell volcanic fires
　　so warm.
But need I take up arms, and plunge within the
　　brother's breast
The hostile sword which once I thought might in
　　its scabbard rest,
Against the dear Palmetto State with maniac rage
　　conspire?
Perish the thought.　I will not wed my memory
　　to fire.
Here, here, I hurl the oath aside, if such its fear-
　　ful sweep.
Sword! sword of Hayne! my father's sword!
　　above thee I could weep.
Forth to the skirmish, forth again, I snap the
　　withes that bind;
Samson himself again, with force Philistia's camp
　　shall find.

*　　*　　*　　*　　*　　*　　*

A skirmish with the scarlet coats, and in the ranks
　　again
Is he, the champion disenthralled, the now re-
　　pentant Hayne.
The deep disgrace is wiped away, the leprous spot
　　is healed;

He shouts his olden battle-songs, "Palmetto in
    the field !"
Steady and firm, a column now of light and hope
    and faith,
He sweeps along with heart of oak, straight on in
    duty's path.
The hand that signed allegiance once to Albion's
    sceptred lord
The vials of the patriot's wrath are freely from it
    poured.
Win back the forfeited estate of name, win back
    the crown,—
The crown of stern integrity, the worthiest renown.
He wins it back, but as the point so lustrous has
    been gained,
A prisoner to the hulk so dark that noble heart is
    chained.
And Rawdon says he will not grant a trial's
    common form
For him, who must prepare to meet the whirl-
    wind and the storm.
Oh, spare him, for his children's sake, they cannot
    spare their sire ;
Oh, spare him, and your name august the muse
    shall give the lyre.
Thronging they come, those missives white, by
    ladies' hands prepared,—
Say, for those moving documents shall Hayne by
    thee be spared ?

Oh, Charleston does not wish to write that gallant
    name in dust :
Rawdon, in thee they yet repose a willing faith
    and trust.

*   *   *   *   *   *   *

Ask not the wolf for mercy : the gibbet looms on
    high ;
The spectral form of Hayne is full against that
    tropic sky.
Rebel and traitor ! such the words which reach
    his dying ear.
Rebel and traitor, didst thou say ? Oh, such
    there is not here.
A soul of truth, a heart of worth, a conscience all
    serene,—
Is such the man to whom belongs an epithet so
    mean ?
No, martyred Hayne ! thy country yet that mem-
    ory will embalm ;
That short career was all redeemed by valor, cool ·
    and calm.
The weakness of the tempted heart we, too, per-
    chance, may know ;
But firmer, fuller loyalty our spirits need not
    show.
If for an interval so brief he could diverge from
    good,
The wrong, retrieving like a man, he purged the
    stain with blood.

THE SAME OLD DRUM.

When the corner-stone of the Bunker Hill Monument was laid, in 1825, General Lafayette, who was then on a visit to this country, was present, and listened with great attention to the splendid oration of the orator of the day, the Hon. Daniel Webster. A great number of Revolutionary heroes were there, and among the rest an old drummer, who, on the heights of Bunker Hill, half a century before, had rallied the scattered columns of the Americans by his vigorous beat. To make the ceremony more impressive, he carried with him *the identical drum* whose notes had fallen on the ear of the lamented General Warren. On that occasion about two hundred Revolutionary soldiers were present, and forty who had participated in the action of Bunker Hill. Webster addressed, it is computed, about fifteen thousand of his assembled countrymen in his most noble and majestic strains. That festal day has never been surpassed in all its collateral circumstances of interest.

THE throng advanced, and 'mid the peal of joy
   The corner-stone was laid on Bunker's height,
Where half a century's sun, in rolling course,
    Had nourished freedom's plant with warmth
      and light.
One eye was there, which in its infant state
   Had watched the progress of the land he loved ;
One arm was there, which steadied truth's own
    ark,
   One heart, whose sympathies had never roved.

August in moral greatness, he had come
    To tread our soil ere being's sun had set ;
Changed in its outward aspect now with age,
    But fresh in soul, the generous Lafayette.
He stood where Warren's blood the sod had
        made
    Rich in its fertile memories, and dear,
And as within its bed the stone reposed,
    He dropped upon its granite form a tear.

And one old man, *whose drum* in Bunker's
        fray
    Had rallied broken columns by its spell,
Was there to linger by the son of France,
    And, garrulous with age, his story tell.
That drum ! *he held it yet*, though fifty years
    Had laid its stirring music all at rest ;
That drum, whose earliest beat a nation heard,
    Now the throned mistress of the mighty West.

The drum that put fresh courage in the heart
    When 'mid the battle surge the standard rose,
Which rolled its tocsin when the spiral flame
    Bespoke fair Charleston vanquished by its
        foes.
Then, with athletic vigor, how he brought
    The lengthened roll responsive to his beat !
And youthful comrades grasped the musket tight,
    And fainting soldiers stood on firmer feet.

No need, old veteran, of thy antique drum ;
　　Here 'tis the relic of those fiercer days,
When on the bayonet the beam of heaven
　　Fell to find beauty in reflected rays.
Peace has put on her snow-white garments
　　　　now,
　　With smiles of love she beckons thee to rest,
And eager nations catch her matron voice,
　　Inviting them to pillow on her breast.

Old drummer of the Revolution, hail !
　　Auspicious was thy presence to the day,
When Webster's mighty accents up the hill
　　Floated in grandeur to the clouds away.
Webster beheld you, and with touch of skill
　　He played upon each sympathetic chord,
Till every feeling roused, you scarce controlled
　　The tempest wakened by his potent word.

Old drummer of the Revolution, hail !
　　The pageant was without thee less in worth ;
And who should be the chosen guest but he
　　Whose heart had memories of the nation's
　　　　birth ?
The monument has risen, but they are gone
　　Who thronged to see that bright inaugural ;
And Lafayette and Daniel Webster sleep,
　　How well, how soundly, in death's silent
　　　　hall !

And the old drummer, too, has laid him down
  In his green hills, like weary child, to rest,
His work accomplished, and fair honor's crown
  Reposing sweetly on his pulseless breast.
Oh, my dear country, let those olden deeds
  Subdue the frenzied rage of party strife,
Lest Discord's drum shall wake a traitor band,
  And rouse the venomed snake, Disunion, into
    life.

THE BARON DE KALB.

The Baron De Kalb, a German in the service of
France, at the battle of Camden, South Carolina, received eleven wounds, which proved fatal. Lieutenant
Du Buysson, his trusty aide-de camp, embracing his
wounded and sinking general, announced his rank and
nation, and, while thus generously exposing himself, he
was wounded and taken prisoner. De Kalb had a pre-
sentiment of the defeat at Camden.

FROM the blue Moselle, where the waters sleep,
In a cradle of sunshine broad and deep,
Where the vine-hills ring with the song of glee,
And the thyme has fragrance for bird and bee ;
From the land of love and beauty's spell
De Kalb, the noble, has come to dwell
In the forest home of the Western wild,
Where Freedom yearns for her way-worn child.

And his is the warm Teutonic blood
Which leaps at the sound of the rushing flood,
And his is the German nerve of steel
Which will not bend at the cannon's peal ;
A heart that clings to the good and true
As the cedar stern, but as mild as dew ;
Stern in its impulse against the wrong,
Mild to the feeble who meet the strong.

Talk to him now of that bloody fray,
When Bunker's height in its glory lay ;
Talk to him now of that freezing night,
When December's stars had a holy light,
When the winds were bleak and the shores were
        bare,
As Washington crossed the Delaware,
And see how his cheek, to his feelings true,
Like a sunset cloud, has a deeper hue.

On the field at last, on the battle-ground,
His heart is up to its noblest bound,
And Camden will tell, on the future page,
Of the blood of youth and the skill of age ;
Of the blood of youth, for De Kalb was young
In the hopes he cherished when tocsins rung ;
Of the skill of age, for De Kalb was wise,
And judgment tempered his sympathies.

Eleven his wounds on that fatal day,
When sabre and sword made clear the way ;
Eleven his wounds when Du Buysson sped
With his master's fate his own to wed.
" Oh, spare the Baron De Kalb !" his cry ;
The plaint went up to the tropic sky,
But the pulse of Britain beat fiercely on,
And her heart was a fragment of the roughest
    stone.

Du Buysson falls to the victor' share,
For such was the issue of filial care ;
And the loyal heart of the baron beat
From the field of mortals its sad retreat.
A stranger died who our cause revered,
In his closing moments by Freedom cheered,
Sounding these words with a blessed tone, —
" The patriot sinks, but the work goes on."

MRS. WASHINGTON IN CAMP.

Mrs. Martha Washington was accustomed to say that,
owing to her yearly residences in the camp during the
winter season, she had heard the first cannon at the
opening and the last at the closing of all the campaigns
in the Revolution.

SHE heard the opening peal
Which ushered in the fray,

When first on Cambridge's noble heights
   The stern encampment lay ;
From blue Potomac's flood,
   From home and its employ,
She travelled with a woman's zeal
   To prove her hero's joy.

When weary men and worn
   At Morristown were placed,
And on their leader's troubled brow
   Sorrow its mark had traced,
New Jersey's hills beheld
   Her fine, majestic form ;
New Jersey's heart her image held
   In its recesses warm.

When Pestilence his wing
   O'er Valley Forge had spread,
The gentle wife was there, amid
   The dying and the dead,
And benisons fell thick
   Where'er her footsteps moved ;
She was the idol of the camp,
   Whose simple name they loved.

When Newburg held the chief,
   By Hudson's flowing tide,
In the old house of Holland form
   She nestled to his side.

At Middlebrook she stood,
   The jewel of the throng,
Where the true wives of Knox and Greene
   Joined in the cheerful song.

When first the shafts of scorn
   From bitter lips were sent,
To soothe her dear one's troubled soul
   Her magic powers were bent ;
And he, the good and true,
   By secret foes beset,
Felt, as he caught her truthful gaze,
   He had an Eden yet.

Oh, ye who shrink from toil,
   Ye maidens of the lute,
Would such privations, doubly stern,
   Your dainty feelings suit ?
Yet such fatigue was borne,
   Until the day was won,
By her who earned the name she bore,
   The Lady Washington.

WASHINGTON'S VISIT TO HIS MOTHER.

After the surrender of Lord Cornwallis at Yorktown, General Washington, accompanied by a splendid retinue, pressed on to Fredericksburg, the residence of his

mother. Then dismissing the attendant train, he went
on foot to her modest mansion, to renew his filial inter-
course and receive her blessing.

MOTHER ! I have sped to greet thee
  From the field of sounding arms,
For my bosom yearned to meet thee
  'Mid the camp and its alarms.
Early days and memories tender
  To my spirit's portals press,
And I must the tribute render
  Of my boyhood's fond caress.

When the ocean-flag that covered
  England's vessels fired my zeal,
O'er my path thy love that hovered
  Could not its regrets conceal ;
And the warrant which my brother
  Had procured me was but vain ;
Naval glory from his mother
  Could not then your George retain.

If thy guardian care had slumbered,
  Freedom might have missed thy son ;
He who years of toil has numbered
  And her final battle won.
Thou didst thus reserve for glory
  Him who longed to tempt the wave,
And perchance from billows hoary
  Didst the heart that loved thee save.

Mother ! we have won the battle ;
   Yorktown tells of grounded arms ;
Pounders now may cease to rattle,
   Tyranny no longer harms.
To our banner, where entwining
   Gleamed the lily crest of France,
Albion crouches, though repining,
   Crouches with a shivered lance.

When by Braddock's side I lingered
   By Monongahela's tide,
And fair Hope, the rosy-fingered,
   Whispered me I was your pride,
Thought I not that laurels greener,
   Issues nobler, sterner yet,
Would in years maturer springing
   Meet thee ere thy sun had set.

With a retinue so splendid
   I have come to Frederick's site,
And by glorious suite attended,
   Feel a throb of keen delight.
Leaving now that guard of honor,
   I would meet thee here alone,
And within the modest mansion
   Only be the widow's son.

Mother ! all the past recalling,
   As by wizard's fairy spell,
Let us talk of little Mildred,
   Sister gone with God to dwell ;

Let us talk of Charles and Betty,
   Linking with them Samuel, John,
Bound a pearly string together
   Ere my father death had won.

Mother ! since to thee is owing
   All my principles of right,
All my faith, so sure and glowing,
   In the long and tedious fight,
Here from Yorktown promptly speeding,
   I would bid thee share my joy,
Just as much thy blessing needing,
   Just as much the widow's boy.

GENERAL WOODHULL.

General Woodhull, after the delivery of his sword, was requested to cry out, "God save the king !" Refusing to obey so degrading a command, he received at each succeeding denial a sabre-cut or a bayonet-thrust. Thus, with his head and body covered with wounds, he was hurried to Jamaica, and exposed to public gaze in the Stone Church. Thence he was transferred to a prison-ship at Gravesend, and finally put on shore, where his arm was amputated, having mortified. His wife accompanied his body to the grave.

SHE bore him over seventy miles
   Of long and weary road,
Beneath September's sunny smiles,
   To nature's last abode.

How had he perished?   Ask the wounds
  So thick upon his frame ;
Oh ! ask the taunting note that sounds
  When Albion breathes his name.

He gave his sword when circling foes
  Cut off the hope of flight ;
But sabre-cuts the hand bestows,
  Unused to honor's plight.
Those sabre-cuts baptized with blood
  The fainting form of him
Who to his creed unbending stood,
  'Mid terrors sternly grim.

He would not say, "God save the king !"
  Nor thus the trust belie,
Which Tory herds were bartering,
  When gibbets loomed on high ;
And thrusts of cutlasses were given
  As silence sealed his tongue,
For pity's golden bond was riven
  Those ruthless hearts among.

Thus hurried to Jamaica fast,
  On foot he bleeding goes ;
The drama deeper shades doth cast
  Ere its stern actings close.
The church becomes his prison now ;
  How could its stones refrain,
As, standing with a gory brow,
  The martyr bears his chain?

111

Thence pressed on board the prison-ship,
    He languished for *her* care,
Who glued to his affection's lips
    And breathed a woman's prayer.
On shore at last, the surgeon's knife
    Brings no relief to him ;
His arm he yielded with his life,
    And Woodhull's eye was dim.

She came ! his own, his tried, his true !
    She watched his latest breath ;
Wiped from his brow the clammy dew,
    And bore him cold in death
O'er seventy miles of weary way,
    To where his kindred dust
Amid sepulchral silence lay,
    In Heaven's kind care and trust.

"God save the king !" That strain has fled
    Far from Columbia's hills ;
Another anthem-peal has spread
    By all our vales and rills.
Woodhull ! the lay thou wouldst not wake
    Though sabre-cuts came free,
Shall never in its cadence break,
    If we have sons like thee !

FIVE DAYS TOO LATE.

Had Cornwallis been able to hold out five days longer, he might possibly have been relieved, for on the 24th of October (he surrendered on the 19th) a British fleet, conveying an army of seven thousand men, arrived off the Chesapeake ; but finding that his lordship had already surrendered, this armament returned to New York and Sandy Hook.

FIVE days too late ! Go steer your fleet
    From Chesapeake's broad bay ;
Ye cannot share a battle's heat,
    Whate'er Sir Henry say.
With folded colors, silent drums,
    Our foe his arms lays down,
Before the boasted succor comes
    To strengthen England's crown.

Five days too late ! He waited long,
    With patient heart and true,
With Clinton ever on his tongue,
    And coming aid in view.
At length despatches whispered doubt ;
    Cornwallis was in gloom ;
The allied forces now were out ;
    He heard their cannon's boom.

Lafayette and Vioménil,
    Two kindred sons of France,
His two redoubts have vanquished well
    With an unbroken lance ;

De Grasse and Rochambeau and Knox,
   A triple strand of Fate,
Have given him electric shocks,
   And ye are all too late.

The " Charon" frigate was on fire,
   The " Transport" owned the flame,
And yet we rebels did not tire,
   And still pursued the game.
From York to Gloucester tried to pass
   The army, faint and worn,
But wind and rain began the chase,
   And it was back by morn.

The God of Battles had decreed
   The net-work should be tight ;
His justice crowned the wond'rous deed,
   And man pronounced it right.
'Twas Heaven delayed you, haughty fleet,
   And made you fold the sail,
Now back to Sandy Hook retreat
   With impulse in the gale.

Yes, York and Gloucester Point shall speak
   Of God's controlling arm,
And tell that human force is weak
   If He protect from harm.

The mighty prey is taken now,
  Freedom unveils her star,
Cornwallis to repinings low
  Has changed his blast of war.

Go, take your brave seven thousand back,
  The succor is in vain ;
Defeat is now upon your track,
  The cause of wrong is slain.
Five days too late ! Go move the keel
  From Chesapeake's blue wave,
Learn that a despot's iron heel
  Is nought, if God will save.

FRANCIS'S TAVERN.

In Francis's tavern, New York, Washington met, on December 4, 1783, the principal officers of the American army. Filling a glass, he said : "With a heart full of love and gratitude, I now take my leave of you. May your future be as prosperous as your past has been glorious." Having drank, he requested them each to advance and take him by the hand. This was done in profound silence. Then, forming themselves into mute procession, they accompanied him to Whitehall, where a barge was in readiness to receive him. He entered it. He took off his hat, respectfully bowed to them, and bade them a silent farewell, when they returned, in the same dignified way, to the tavern.

He raised the goblet to his lips,
  And ere he drained the tide,
As if their joys were in eclipse,
  His trusty warriors sighed.
He pledged them in the ruddy stream
  With faltering voice and slow ;
His eye with moisture dimmed its beam,
  For heroes grief may show.

" Brothers in arms ! a long farewell,   .
  Rent is the silken tie,
And here our bosoms heave and swell
  In parting company.
In bivouac and council-tent,
  And with the charging file,
Each to the other comfort lent,
  The aiding hand, the smile.

" Our standard ! centre of our joys,
  Its every shred was dear,
And ease and gold we counted toys
  Compared with soldiers' cheer ;
And when our country breathed our name
  With feeling deep and true,
The vision of an honest fame
  Our weakened fancy drew.

" Brothers in arms ! on history's page
  Those blazing deeds shall stand,
And Valley Forge the thoughts engage,
  And nerve our children's hand.

" Yes, Bennington and Eutaw Springs,
  ♦And Monmouth with its tale,
Will greet the ears of Europe's kings
  To make the cheek grow pale.

" Brothers in arms ! the grave has won
  Its trophies from our side,
And Custis sleeps, my cherished son,
  My beauty and my pride ;
Hundreds whose hearts beat full and high,
  When Charleston felt the brand,
Have joined the heroes in the sky,
  In heaven's unfettered land.

" Oh, sainted dead ! and did ye know
  When Yorktown's grounded arms
Told of the last decisive blow
  That hushed the hearts' alarms ?
Oh, Woodhull, Warren, Wooster ! say
  If, when our flag was high,
'Mid glory's blaze ye caught its ray
  And felt its influence nigh ?

" Brothers in arms ! our homes will greet
  Their masters on return ;
Dear ones will come with quickened feet
  And love's pure incense burn.

117

" Then tell them of that guiding Hand,
    That clear directing power,   •
That led our Macedonian band
    To victor's final hour.

" Come each and give the truthful grasp,
    Come lock your hands in mine ;
Brothers in arms ! one final clasp
    Above this pledge of wine ;
Your past ! Fame claims it as her dower ;
    Your future ! Peace will share ;
Go, and may God His blessings shower,
    And make you each His care."

The hands were locked, the pledge was given,
    The waiting barge appears ;
He stepped aboard, the tie was riven
    In silence and in tears.
My country ! bind them to thy breast,
    Those sons who parted then,
For they who gave devotion's test
    Were patriots and were men !

WASHINGTON RESIGNING HIS COMMISSION.

On the 23d of December, 1783, in presence of a numerous company of spectators, General Washington resigned his commission into the hands of Congress, then assembled at Annapolis, Maryland.

TAKE back the trust, my country, here
  The power reverts to thee ;
I come with conscience, fair and clear,
  To earn a good degree.
'Mid care and toil my weary heart
  Has longed to see the day
When office and myself should part,
  Ere all my locks were gray.

Take my commission ! When 'twas given,
  I said I was content
To fight till all our chains were riven,
  Nor ask emolument.
And, oh ! the smiles and tears which blend
  Around my vision now,
Here make my grateful thanks ascend,
  That I have kept my vow.

Let others fancy, if they can,
  The current of my bliss,
When murmuring praises swiftly ran
  Through old Annapolis.

I felt that payment came in full
  For stern campaigns and long ;
I felt that doubly beautiful
  Was that approving song.

Fathers ! I thank you for the trust,
  Which joyously I yield,
For mine was not ambition's lust,
  Though beckoned to the field ;
And glad am I that peace at last
  Becomes the envied boon
Of those who heard the bugle-blast,
  And bore the heat of noon.

Take back the trust ; I long to press
  My threshold once again,
When good old neighbors throng to bless
  The reunited chain.
My spear to ploughshare let me turn,
  My sword to pruning-hook,
And as the simple farmer learn
  From nature's teeming book.

Take back the trust, and say that I
  Have earned a good degree ;
Let my dear country testify
  That she was all to me.

She knows I come with conscience clear,
  With calm, approving breast,
To leave my tried commission here,
  And pass away to rest.

TREATIES OF AMITY.

The independence of the United States was acknowl-
edged by Sweden on the 5th of February, 1783 ; by Denmark on the 25th ; by Spain on the 24th of March, and
by Russia in July. Treaties of amity and commerce
were also concluded with each of these powers.

SHE stands erect before the powers of earth,
  To claim their sanction and their meed receive :
And Europe's sovereigns, to attest her worth,
  Hasten with hers *their* names to interweave.
For they have heard of all that sanguine strife
  Which roused the granite purpose of her will,
And how at last, with scarcely rescued life,
  She to the future looks, all hopeful still.

She stands erect before the powers of earth,
  Girding her loins for glory's lustrous crown.
And as she flings her gorgeous ensign forth,
  The elder nations her fair birthright own ;
They come to grasp her hand with love and truth,
  To form the league her interest which seals,
And catch from her the ardent glow of youth,
  Which, as they hail her, to their bosom steals.

And first old Sweden, where Adolphus ruled.
   Monarch who right espoused and held it fast,
Whose mind and heart by discipline were
      schooled,
   Mild as the zephyr, stern 'mid war's loud blast.
Old Sweden, with her boreal lights aglow,
   Hailed the new star whose virgin disk appeared,
And Denmark came, a fostering arm to throw
   Around the pillar now by freedom reared.

Spain, too, where Charles and Philip, sire and son,
   Held the firm rein beneath the tropic sky,
Beheld what God by Washington had done,
   And hastened all her joy to testify.
And Russia, whose imperial Peter stood
   In bold relief upon her infant page,
Prepared to canonize the great and good,
   And in the work of amity engage.

From Elsinore to where the Escurial pile
   Told of the sacred dust of chivalry,
Through Europe's length, the continent and isle,
   Rang the bold deeds of her who now was free.
Monmouth and Saratoga had their spell
   From Stockholm to the Adriatic main,
And by the blue Garonne could children tell
   How Britain wept beside her sundered chain.

And when America uprose at last
  To challenge homage from the gazing throng,
And Yorktown's fame to burning history passed,
  There filled her ear a swell of generous song ;
For even kings had marked her onward stride,
  Her alternating phases to the goal,
And when she gained it felt an honest pride,
  And in their treaties threw an ardent soul.

Oh ! my dear country, how thy pulses beat
  When thou 'mid sovereign nations took thy
      place !
The price was weighty, but the gain was sweet,
  Blooming the crown, though long and hard the
      race.
Begun in fears, continued in suspense,
  The fight for truth had closed 'mid joyous
      peals ;
And as thou marked thy fair inheritance,
  To thy moist lid is it a tear-drop steals ?

Yes, tears of gratitude become thee now,
  With wider sway and more exalted name,
With coronet upon thy matron brow,
  And history wedded to eternal fame.
Oh ! stand, my country, by Potomac's wave,
  Where sleeps thy Father in his tomb august,
And there a blessing from his spirit crave
  Upon thy mighty charge, thy more than hal-
      lowed trust.

THE REGIMENT OF TEN.

The citizens of Alexandria, when convened, constituted the first public company in America which had the pleasure of pouring a libation to the prosperity of the ten States which had actually adopted the general government.—*Washington's letter to Pinkney, June 28, 1788.*

PINKNEY! the tenth has signed the bond, ten
 Sovereign States have come ;
No sweeter music have they found than Federal
 fife and drum ;
Ten links are forged, and yet the chain a mightier
 band shall own,
Successive States shall grasp the pen when Union's
 worth is known,
Objections melting like the snow beneath an April
 beam.
One mighty front our land shall show, nor riven
 fragments seem ;
Old Alexandria sent her chime in merry notes afar,
When our Virginia, true to time, burst a new-risen
 Star.
Pinkney ! we poured libations out such as no
 Grecian knew,
And Athens had no blended shout like our huzzas
 so true ;
Rockets have burst and jovial cheer the holiday
 has told,
Would that my Pinkney had been here our revels
 to behold.

Not Yorktown with surrendered host, its banners
    and its men,
Has proved to me so proud a boast as those sur-
    rendered ten
Our Constitution, like a bride, arrayed in purest
    sheen,
Has come for shelter to our side while on her
    breast we lean.
That Federal bond ! my spirit leaps to trace the
    future good
Which in its every section sleeps, though yet
    scarce understood,
Evolving blessings year by year, dissension may
    not spring,
When to our people's hearts so clear its cherished
    mandates ring.
Pinkney ! not Colonies, but States, sovereign yet
    banded powers,
With circling arms, like joyous mates, shall dance
    away the hours ;
A Covenant of Salt shall prove the league our
    people make,
And others of that feast of love shall one by one
    partake,
Nor shall be wanting men of truth in blissful
    years to come
To vindicate its every clause and strike foul Treason
    dumb ;

The comments of the wise and great upon its text
    shall be
Like fringe of blue on Jewish robe, to grace its
    symmetry ;
And all our thousands in their tents, when days
    are growing dark,
Shall turn their eyes, one blended gaze, towards its
    Radiant Ark.
Then help me to a note of joy, old Alexandria cries,
The little one who finds his toy has not such ec·
    stasies.
We want that Oriental band of sackbut, harp, and lute
To grace an epoch so august and aid Columbia's
    flute ;
But, dearest Pinkney, ere I start my ploughshare
    to its task,
Your close attention to my toast I very freely ask.
Then I will moderate my warmth in farmer's toil
    again,
And sink the Federal Covenant in leagues of oats
    and grain :
" Here's to the heads so cool and calm, on future
    good intent,
Who framed with caution, yet with zeal, the
    honored instrument ;
Here's to the signers of the chart, here's to their
    golden pen,
Here's to the States, now one in heart, *that Regi-
    ment of Ten.*"

ADMINISTER THE OATH.

ADMINISTER the oath, and give the reins to up-
    right hands ;
And let our country take her place amid the scep-
    tered lands ;
Without a royal coronet, nor purple-cinctured
    limb,
'Mid all the princely brotherhood, oh ! who eclipses
    him ?

Within the open gallery, his look serene and calm,
While Freedom with a new-strung lyre stands by
    to wake the psalm,
He waits to pledge his honest word that faithful
    he will prove,
Nor from integrity depart, nor from the right re-
    move.

Oh ! Chancellor, that bond apart, his spirit would
    not swerve,
The Constitution he would still a holy trust pre-
    serve ;
His life has been a sacrifice, knit to the altar's
    horn,
And his can be no blemished age who had so pure
    a morn.

Hark ! the loud swell of manly notes,—well may
    the air be rent,
A lustrous drama he begins, their honored Presi-
    dent ;
And mighty issues he beholds with clear, anointed
    eye,
Evolving, while his country solves, the problem
    Liberty.

Look on him ! see, his locks are gray, but how
    erect his form!
Ah ! he has known the iron hail of many a battle-
    storm,
And he has crossed on Christmas-eve, when forest-
    trees were bare,
With that old Continental coat, the frozen Dela-
    ware.

Soon shall the Senate and the House his counsels
    sage receive,
Who for the Cabinet profound the stirring camp
    can leave,
Alike at home with pen or sword, so fortune blest
    decrees,
In war a Cæsar, and in peace a thoughtful Socrates.

The cannon ye have heard to-day, it had no tone
    of Mars,
Ye are no slaves by tyrants kept to peep through
    golden bars ;

No chartered wrongs impose the yoke and deck
    that yoke with gems,
To make you fondle what you hate and kiss their
    diadems.

The Government you honor now, what is it but
    your choice,
The fig-tree planted by your hands, beneath it ye
    rejoice,
And every shout of ecstasy that through the welkin
    rings,
Shows that your axe has cleared away the upas
    growth of kings.

'Twas April when at Lexington the martyr-blood
    flowed fast,
And through your borders loudly pealed that
    resurrection blast ;
'Tis April now, but Flora's crown, unwet by
    crimson dew,
Settles in beauty and in balm on him the good and
    true.

Look on him ! oh, his mother's heart is beating
    fast to-day,
This crowning rapture is her own ere she has past
    away ;

The truthful boy, the active man, the Chief to
    warfare bent,
The conqueror with Yorktown's bays, and now the
    President.

THE FIRST CABINET.

" At the head of the Department of State he placed
Thomas Jefferson ; at the head of the Treasury, Alex-
ander Hamilton ; at the head of the War Department,
General Knox ; in the office of Attorney-General, Ed-
mund Randolph ; and at the head of the Judicial Department, Mr. Jay. Thus the *first Cabinet* was fully
organized."

THE Ship of State must sail,
But to woo a prosperous gale ;
Stout hearts and ready hands
Must carry out commands
    On the deck.
They must know the screw-bolts well,
Each inch of cordage tell,
When the yard-arms to square,
Or scud with poles all bare,
    Lest she wreck.

The captain has his eye
Full fixed upon the sky,
To watch its fitful look ;
The firmament, his book,
    Must be scanned.

A cargo rich as gems,
For it the flood he stems,
And the ocean's highway keeps
Where no Maelstrom current sweeps
    Either hand.

Ere she launches free and full,
And like child let loose from school,
Plunges forth into the tide,
With hilarity and pride,
    From the dock,
Oh ! tell us every name
Which is coupled with her fame !
They who to time go down,
As the treasures of renown
    They unlock !

See, Jefferson, the sage,
And Hamilton engage,
To use their naval lore,
While Knox imparts his store,
    Kind of heart.
Now Randolph link with Jay,
For 'tis time to launch away ;
Your ensign's in the breeze,
And Freedom's melodies
    Cheer your start !

That mighty Ship of State
Must Jehovah's succor wait,
Or her Cabinet complete
May dissension's tempest meet,
    And disperse.
Oh ! seek his sheltering wing,
As to Washington you cling ;
And as you gain the shore,
A blessing He will pour,
    Not a curse.

THE CLOSING LYRIC.

The happiness of America is intimately connected with the happiness of all mankind. She will become the safe and respected asylum of virtue, integrity, toleration, equality, and tranquil happiness.—*Lafayette's letter to his wife, May 30, 1777.*

WHEN in the past I longed to sweep the lyre,
  My thoughts ranged freely o'er the deeds of
    Fame,
And though it seemed presumption to aspire
  To throw a halo round my country's name,
Yet did I hope to sing of those bright deeds,
  Compared to which Thermopylæ was dull,
Though mine were pipings on a shepherd's reed,
  More earnest than ornate, more true than beau-
    tiful.

And true to that old instinct, I have sung
 Dear Freedom's onward march for toilsome
  years,
From where at Concord the vast mine was sprung,
 To where at Yorktown we entombed our fears.
And often as I traced the devious path,
 The labyrinthine maze my fathers trod,
And saw the despot with his scowl of wrath,
 I felt my country's stay, her only prop was God.

When first I rolled a lyric from the chord,
 And told of Warren, martyred in his prime,
My father lived to praise each ardent word,
 And glow at hearing deeds of olden time.
And often as I read the sounding line
 His bosom swelled and tear-drops gathered free,
For Putnam's name with him was but divine,
 And Stony Point brought up the deeds of An-
  thony.

Now, as I close the simple lyric strain,
 He is not here to crown my task complete,
For his warm eulogy I look in vain ;
 No more he springs the stanza warm to greet.
He whose own ancestor was in the fray ;
 He whose first teachings were of all the brave,
Whose love of country never knew decay,
 Is with his fathers now, a tenant of the grave.

My little offering laid on Freedom's shrine,
  My simple lyrics may oblivion find,
But the pure wreath my fingers loved to twine
  May be preserved as a memento kind.
Some rural hearth may garner up my song,
  Some lovely maiden in her scrap-book place
Those heartfelt numbers which were borne along
    In rough heroic strength, though wanting oft in
      grace.

My country ! glorious, happy, and secure,
  Write Bunker Hill, the blazon of thy shield,
And that dear guardian, Washington the pure,
  Be thy true crest upon an azure field.
Think of the past, its wrongs, its tale of woe,
  Think of the huts of logs where patriots dwelt,
Think how ere Freedom struck the final blow
    Her God she did invoke and at His footstool
      knelt.

Then with thy memory stored with noble deeds,
  Stretch thy broad arms to clasp each ocean wide,
And vow that he from honor who recedes
  Shall be to foul contempt and scorn allied.
Be thine the flag which knows no spot nor stain,
  Be thine the sword which flashed at Eutaw
      Springs,
And throned upon thy mountains shalt thou reign
    When diadems are dust and time has swallowed
      kings.